Surprise … Swipe Right

Surprise... Swipe Right

A Big Easy Holiday Comedy

RHONDA M. LAWSON

Published by
Meet the World Image Solutions
www.mtwimagesolutions.com

For permissions contact:
info@mtwimagesolutions.com

Cover design by Dr. Rhonda M. Lawson
Printed in the United States of America

ISBN: 979-8-9988626-2-5

Other fiction by Rhonda M. Lawson

Cheatin' in the Next Room

A Dead Rose

Putting It Back Together

Some Wounds Never Heal

Twylite

Trust

A New Renaissance: A Celebration of African American Fiction

Reader Reactions

This love story gave me hope again! We all deserve love regardless of age or whatever traumatic experiences we've experienced.
— *Torrie Q. Jones*
Author, Reborn the Book series

The story is really about growth and change, but it never feels heavy. Loretta is such a fun character. She's in for a big surprise that makes the whole book more engaging (and a little spicy, too!).
— *Nicole Butler*
@Butlersbookbag

*To my mother, Phyllis Jones, whose strength shaped me
into the woman I am today.*

*And to every senior reading this story, may this be your reminder
that it is never too late to love, laugh, and dream again.*

Acknowledgments

Believe it or not, this is my first time writing a holiday story. I wanted this story to be a feel-good experience, free of political or racial commentary, and free of violence, games, or negativity. I also wanted to give seniors a story that showed them they were seen and understood. Finally, I wanted to give you a new and fun holiday love story.

This story is rooted in a real-life moment. At one time, I, myself, attempted to put my mom on a dating app. The results weren't nearly as hilarious as the story you're about to read, but I always wondered what would happen if we'd gone all the way with the profile. If you've been following me for a while, you'll know I love to write from the *what-if* factor. In this case, *what if* the dating app had succeeded? What if my mom had found love that started with a secret dating profile?

I had such a great time writing this story, laughing out loud with each joke, tongue-in-cheek comment, and key situation. I hope you'll enjoy reading it just as much.

I'm also deeply grateful for the love and support from my friends and family throughout the course of writing this book.

I thank my community of authors, who inspire me to keep writing, even when I don't feel like it, and my community of readers, who encourage me each day when they remind me of how my stories have touched them. Whether you've attended a workshop, supported the *Black History Month Literary Weekend*, tuned into *Horizons Author Lounge*, or simply sent a kind message, you've helped keep this pen in my hand and this fire in my spirit.

To the *Meet the World Image Solutions* family: Thank you for walking this literary journey with me. Whether we've worked together once or on multiple projects, you are part of something bigger than I could have ever imagined. I pray you'll stay on this journey with me because there's much more to come!

And now, without any further delay, let's get into this story. May it remind you that love is still on the horizon, no matter your age!

Blessings and Happy Holidays,
Dr. Rhonda

Chapter 1

"Every year you ask me the same thing, and every year I say no," Loretta said with a laugh as she picked through a box of Christmas decorations in search of her favorite silver glitter ornaments. "One of these days you're gonna get tired of asking."

"Nope, because one day you're gonna listen," Liza replied, raising her eyebrows. Without looking up, she grabbed two silver ornaments from her mother's pile and hung them on the Douglas fir.

Loretta cut her eyes at her daughter and smirked, half irritated, half amused. They went through the same song and dance every Christmas. She loved Liza, and appreciated that her daughter wanted her to be happy, but why couldn't Liza understand that she *was* happy?

"I'm just saying, Momma," Liza said, snatching more ornaments and hanging them on the tree, "how do you always give the best New Year's Eve party and never have a date?"

"Because I'm the host!" Loretta snapped, snatching an ornament from her daughter just before she could hang it. "I don't have time to entertain a date. And you were about to put that ornament too close to the last one."

"You didn't have to snatch it," Liza scolded. She smiled wickedly. "And by midnight, no one needs a host. You just need a little lovin'."

"Girl, watch ya' mouth! I'm still ya' momma!"

Liza snorted and turned back to the decoration box. Loretta playfully shook her head and inspected the tree, moving a few ornaments that hadn't been strategically placed. She had grown used to correcting Liza's work. No one understood the art of decorating a Christmas tree like Loretta. Really, no one cared the way she did, and she was okay with that.

"Grams," a youthful voice called from the other room. Loretta turned just in time to see twenty-year-old Maya walk into the living room. "Can I make some hot chocolate?"

"Why aren't you helpin' with this tree?" Loretta asked, rolling her eyes. "Talkin' 'bout some hot chocolate."

"Grams, you know you don't like how anybody decorates that tree," Maya replied with a laugh. "I'm surprised you're lettin' Mom help you."

"I'm a glutton for punishment," Liza said just as Loretta snatched a roll of tinsel from her hands. "Dang, Momma!"

"Sorry," Loretta said with a chuckle. "I'm just not ready for that yet. I have an idea for the lights I wanna try. Somethin' I saw on TikTok."

"*You're* on TikTok?" Maya sneered.

"Um, yes, Ms. Smarty," Loretta retorted, dropping the tinsel and placing her hands on her hips. "Your grandmother ain't *that* old."

"I'm not sayin' you're old," Maya tried to explain. "It's just that you don't see a whole lot of ol—I mean grandmas on there."

"You'd be surprised. And I heard you almost call me old," Loretta said, playfully swatting at her granddaughter.

Liza laughed and sat in the nearby armchair. "Maya, tell your grandmother she needs to get on TikTok and find herself a date for her party this year."

"That really wouldn't be a bad idea," Maya agreed.

Loretta's eyes widened as she shook her head in exasperation. "Child, go make your hot chocolate and get outta grown folks' business!"

An explosion of laughter filled the living room as Maya scampered back to the kitchen. Loretta loved her family. And even though all their talk about getting her a man was exhausting, she had to admit the banter was fun. It made her house feel alive.

Deep down, she understood why her daughter wanted her to meet someone. It had been five years since her husband James had died of a heart attack. He was only sixty-five, which seemed too young for heart problems, but honestly, they weren't eating right back then. New Orleans cuisine was rich, and they ate it to the fullest. Red beans and rice. Etouffee. Fried chicken. And the shrimp, oyster, and hot sausage po' boys, but only from the gas station down the street. No one in New Orleans went to a fancy restaurant for a po' boy sandwich. The real flavor came from the gas stations and the corner stores.

Loretta and James loved going out, but she also loved to cook. Loretta took pride in preparing homecooked meals for her family. Although she had a full-time job as a teacher, she loved going home and preparing a good meal. Sunday and holiday meals were always spent at her home. It was how she showed her love.

That thought process had to change when James was diagnosed with high blood pressure. Her pressure wasn't much lower, but she was the only one who was willing to make at least a few changes. She cut down on the grease and salt, but those were changes James refused to agree with.

"We need flavor in this house," he used to say.

She had to agree. As much as she wanted to eat healthier, a salad wasn't nearly as tasty as a hot sausage on French bread with a Big Shot pineapple soda on the side. And who wanted a banana when her world-famous pound cake was in the kitchen?

Sadly, it was too late when James finally agreed to the changes. His blood pressure had gotten worse. Loretta finally convinced him to take walks with her, but between the rich food, the drinking, and his career as a construction worker, his heart gave in. Gone at sixty-five.

James's death was a wakeup call for Loretta. She knew she had to get serious about losing weight, so she instantly made healthy switches in her diet and amped up her walks to five miles three times a week. Eventually, she joined a gym and hired a personal trainer. She even changed her diet, saving her rich meals and pound cakes for holidays.

Two years later, she was down thirty pounds, and her A1C had dropped to the normal range. She looked younger, felt healthier, and had begun really enjoying her retirement.

Some might say all that was left was a companion, but she didn't feel she needed one. With church, sorority activities, her family, and occasional travel, she was good. Somebody's old daddy would just get in the way, and she didn't think she could go through taking care of another dying man. She wasn't even sure how many healthy unmarried men her age even existed!

"What time is David comin' to pick y'all up?" Loretta asked, flopping into the armchair.

"You gettin' tired of us?" Liza asked as she returned the leftover decorations to the box.

"Not at all. You know you're always welcome at your momma's house."

"Awww, I love you, too," Liza said, walking to her mother with outstretched arms. Loretta happily accepted her daughter's embrace. "But to answer your question, he should be rolling up pretty soon. We have to stop at the store to get a few more things for Christmas dinner."

"Oh, good," Loretta said, popping up from the chair. "I need to do the same thing. There's a seafood sale, so I need to stock up on some shrimp for the gumbo and stuffed peppers."

"You still want us to make the mac and cheese, right?"

Loretta cut her eyes at Liza. "As long as y'all make it right. Remember, no experimenting on the holidays. Y'all can keep that five-cheese lobster mac you tried to pass off on me for the Fourth of July."

"What do you mean?" Liza asked innocently. "It was good."

"Um, Mom," Maya interjected, walking back into the living room and handing Loretta a mug of steaming hot chocolate, "I gotta be honest. That mac and cheese wasn't all that."

"Maya!" Loretta exclaimed. "I thought you said you liked it?"

She smiled and bit her lip. "I, uh, didn't want to hurt your feelings?"

"Wooooowwww!" Liza sang. "Betrayed by my own child."

"Sorry, Mom. The chicken was good, though."

"I guess."

Loretta chuckled just as the doorbell rang. "That must be David there."

Liza walked to the door and opened it, welcoming her husband with open arms.

"Hey, Momma Loretta!" he greeted before giving her a kiss on the cheek. "The tree is lookin' good."

"It's gonna look better when I string the lights, but I can't do it 'til y'all leave," Loretta said.

"Why?" Maya asked.

"Because it's a surprise, Ms. Nosy," Loretta replied with a smile.

"It's just lights," Maya said dismissively before taking a sip from her hot chocolate.

"Not the way I plan on doing them."

"This, I've got to see," Liza said.

"You will," Loretta said. "You just remember what I said about that mac and cheese."

"She still hasn't forgotten about the Fourth of July fiasco, huh?" David said, smirking.

Liza's head snapped toward her husband. "You, too?"

"Sorry, babe," he said. "You can't trust every YouTube recipe."

"That's cold," Liza replied, feigning sadness.

"Awww, babe, don't feel bad. The collard greens were good."

"Well, I guess between the chicken and greens, I didn't poison y'all too bad."

The living room again filled with laughter as David, Liza, and Maya walked to the front door.

"Do you want me to help you put these decorations away?" David offered, eyeing the box in the middle of the floor.

"No, not yet," Loretta replied. "I'm gonna play with the lights. If you wanna swing by tomorrow, you can put them away then."

"You better have a masterpiece planned the way you're talkin'," Liza said.

"You'll see," Loretta replied. "Now, y'all get on outta here. I need to get a walk in before it gets too dark out. I'll just go to the store for my few groceries tomorrow mornin'."

"That reminds me," Liza said, walking toward her mother. "I meant to ask you. You're cooking for Christmas *and* New Year's Eve?"

"No, just Christmas," Loretta said. "I'm hiring a caterer this year for the New Year's Eve party, but you know I'ma still cook a couple things. You know I only go all out with cooking during the holidays, but since there's more people coming this year, I figured I'd make it easy on myself."

"That makes sense," David agreed. "Just as long as you still make the pound cake and eggnog. None of that store-bought stuff."

"Now you know better than that," Loretta said with a laugh. "I haven't had store-bought eggnog in years. I wouldn't even know how it tastes, so I'm not about to risk being run out of town serving y'all that mess."

"One day, you're gonna teach me how to make it," Maya said.

"I'll make a small batch for Christmas," Loretta said. "You can help me make it then."

"Cool!" Maya exclaimed.

"Who all do you have comin this year?" Liza asked.

"I invited a few of my sorors and their husbands over, along with our usual cousins and some friends," Loretta said. "I think you know most everyone. Mavis is definitely comin'. I also invited Pete and his family."

"All those couples coming and you're gonna be hosting alone," Liza remarked.

"Girl, if you don't leave me alone!" Loretta snapped.

"I'm just sayin', Ma," Liza whined. "You're beautiful, successful … Why shouldn't you have a date every once in a while?"

"Because most people my age aren't out there looking for men," Loretta said. "We're too old for that. What? We supposed to go to the club or something?"

"I'm not sayin' that, but—"

David laid his hand on his wife's shoulder and cut in. "I think your momma made her point."

"I don't know," Maya said, placing her empty mug on the coffee table. "I kind of agree with Mom. I think it would be cute for Grams to go on a date."

"Girl, get out my house," Loretta snapped, again stuck between laughter and irritation. Her family was relentless, but she still loved them all the same.

Maya giggled as she walked out to the car, followed by David and Liza. Loretta walked behind them and waved.

"I'ma see y'all tomorrow," she said.

Liza walked back and hugged her mother again. "I'm sorry for putting you on the spot. I just want you to be happy."

"Baby, I *am* happy. Trust me."

"If you say you are, I'll trust that you are."

* * *

"I don't believe her," Liza told David as they lay in bed later that night. They were supposed to be watching a Christmas movie on BET+, but instead of entertaining her, it only made her think more about her mother.

"I think you're getting a little obsessed, babe," David replied. "Your momma said she's good."

Liza sat up and adjusted the satin bonnet that covered her back-length knotless braids. "Of course, she said she's good. That's what she does. She puts everyone else first and then claims she's good. When Daddy died, she didn't want us fussin' over her, so she said she was good. When we came back to New Orleans and there was only one grocery store open in the entire city and the streetlights weren't workin' yet, she didn't want Maya to be scared so she said she was good. Let's not even talk about when we evacuated. Sittin' in Houston, not knowing a soul, and of course

Momma said she was good. This is what mommas – especially Black mommas – do. I've even found myself doing the same thing with Maya. I'm good, even if secretly, on the inside, I'm not so good."

David sighed and wrapped his arm around his wife. She lay her head on his shoulder, grateful for his comforting gesture.

"Babe, I understand how you feel," he said. "I know you want the best for Momma Loretta. We all want our parents to be happy, but we can't make them do what we want them to do. It sounds like her mind is made up."

"I know. I just wish I knew some eligible old men I could set her up with."

David chuckled. "Now how would you know some senior citizen bachelors?"

Liza smiled. "I'll bet I could find some single seniors if I tried."

David laughed harder. "The only thing you know about Cupid is the Cupid Shuffle, and you just learned to do that!"

That comment earned him a love tap with her pillow. "I can't stand you sometimes."

Chapter 2

Hey, Momma," Liza greeted as she slid on a pair of spandex workout pants. She bent at the waist, giving her back and thighs a deep stretch.

"Mornin', baby," Loretta voice replied, her voice filling Liza's bedroom from the speaker on Liza's phone. "Kinda early, huh?"

"Christmas is only a few days away," Liza said as she tied her shoes. "I still have some runnin' around to do before we swing back your house later on."

"Yeah, about that," Loretta said slowly. "You mind comin' tomorrow instead of today?"

Liza stared at her phone as if her mother were in the room. "Why? What's wrong? You okay?"

Loretta laughed. "Get the concern out your voice. I'm fine. I just have some runnin' around of my own to do today, and I have to finish the decorations."

"Why you tryna do all that yourself, Ma?"

"Who said I was doin' it myself? Pete's comin' over later to help me with the decorations."

"Now, why are you payin' a handyman to do work that your family can do for free?"

"Liza, you just said you had runnin' around to do today. You don't have time to be helpin' me. Besides, I told you I wanted to surprise you."

"You and your surprises," Liza retreated, shaking her head. She walked to her floor-length mirror and inspected her figure. She could lose a couple pounds, but overall, not too bad. She adjusted her outfit and ran her fingers through her braids.

"Uumm!" David's voice came from behind before she could say another word. "That's my chocolate thang, right there."

"And hello to you, son-in-law," Loretta's voice broke in, her voice filling the room like the voice of God. Liza doubled over in laughter.

David jumped as if struck by lightning. "Oh, uh, hey, Momma Loretta. I didn't know you were on the phone."

"Obviously," Loretta replied. She didn't laugh, but there was no obvious anger in her voice.

"My apologies. No disrespect intended," David said, nodding at the phone.

"I know. It's all right. I used to be young and dumb, too," Loretta said, a shadow of a smile in her voice.

Once Liza finally recovered from her laughter, she straightened up and flopped on the bed next to her phone. "Alright, Momma. If you insist on doing it all yourself—well, you and Pete—I guess we'll just check on you later. What time is he coming by?"

"About two. That's why I'm about to get up from here and get my little business done. I want to be home before he gets here."

"Makes sense," Liza agreed. "Well, I'ma let you go so you can get started. We need to get goin', too."

After mother and daughter said their goodbyes, Liza looked at her husband and smiled. He was still standing there with his arms folded, shaking his head. "You are so silly."

"You've gotta warn people when you're talkin' to your momma on speaker," he said with a chuckle.

"How was I supposed to know you were gonna come in here all freaky deaky?"

"Have you seen you in that outfit?" he asked with a wicked smile. He took his wife's hand and twirled her around like a dancer. "Lookin' good, baby."

She wrinkled her nose and shot him a cheesy grin. "Thank you, baby."

David looked toward their bedroom door. "Your daughter up yet?"

"She better be," Liza replied, also looking toward the door. "I told her I was gonna need her help today."

David cut his eyes at her and twisted his mouth in disbelief. "You know that girl is still sleep. It's seven-thirty in the morning on a Saturday."

Liza raised her eyebrows in agreement and walked to the door. She stuck her head out into the hallway and yelled, "MAYA!!"

A few seconds later, they heard faint, sleepy, "I'm up!"

"Girl, you have fifteen minutes!"

"Alright, Mom!"

Liza walked back to the bed shaking her head. She sat next to David and lay her head on his shoulder. "What are we gonna do with that child?"

"The same thing our mothers did with us," he replied, caressing her thigh. "She's gonna be alright. She's only twenty."

"A lazy twenty."

David laughed. "I guess you used to walk barefoot to school five miles each way."

Liza chuckled and playfully elbowed him in the stomach. "I'm not saying that. I'm just saying my parents taught me at a young age to be self-sufficient. I was cleaning the house and cooking my own breakfast at ten years old. By the time I was fourteen, I was making dinner when my parents had to work late. I even started helping Momma with her famous holiday meals. And let's not forget I started my first job on my sixteenth birthday. We've spoiled that girl."

"Different times, different circumstances," David said. He tapped his wife's thigh and rose from the bed. "We never required her to get a job, and you always kick her out of the kitchen while you're cooking. I'm sure your momma didn't do that."

"She didn't, but that was because I didn't play around on Instagram while Momma was cookin'," Liza protested. "If social media were a job, Maya would be rich by now."

"Who says it *can't* be a job? Some of these influencers are making millions and all they're doing is dancing or wrapping rubber bands around watermelons."

Liza laughed and lifted her eyebrows in thought. "That's true. Maybe we can talk to Maya about channeling all that screentime into something productive."

"You know your daughter is pre-med, right? I would say she's focused. We can't just look at what we *think* they should be doing. She works hard in school, so I really don't care that she's sleeping her winter break. Now, I do agree she should get a job, but she's not *you*."

Liza bucked her eyes. "What do you mean, not me?"

"Now baby, you know you're a workaholic. It was like an act of Congress to get you to take these couple days off. Everyone's not built the same way."

Liza nodded. "I get it. But she still doesn't need to be sleeping the day away."

A few minutes later, Maya waltzed into her parents' bedroom fully dressed with her shoulder-length hair in an amazing twist-out. Liza was always amazed at how quickly her daughter could do her hair.

"You look cute," Liza complimented, nodding in approval. She checked her nightstand clock. Maya was five minutes late, but at least she was ready.

"Thank you!" Maya said. "I tried this new cornrow technique I saw on IG last night. You have to blow-dry your hair first, and then cornrow it with curling cream. I wasn't sure how it would look this morning, but it turned out cute. And it's really soft."

"Listen to you sounding like a hair guru," Liza said.

"What's a hair guru?" David asked.

Liza and Maya looked at him and laughed.

"You wouldn't understand," Maya said. "It's an influencer who has mastered the art of doing hair. I call them naturalistas."

David scrunched his eyebrows. "Natcha what?"

Maya laughed again. "Never mind."

"Alright, naturalista, you ready to hit the road?" Liza asked, finally rising from the bed. "We've got a lot to do today."

"Yes, Ma'am," Maya said, backing toward the bedroom door. "And just so you'll know. I heard what you said about me sleeping the day away. It's only eight o'clock. That's hardly a full day."

Liza shook her head as she followed her daughter out of the room. "Child, if I hadn't woken you up, it would have been after one before you emerged from that room!"

* * *

"Pete!" Loretta shouted, placing her hands on her hips with a proud smile. "I think I did it!"

The young handyman speed walked into the living room, rubbing his calloused fingers through his curly hair. When he laid eyes on the tree, he smiled in awe. "Miss Loretta, you did that! That looks good!"

They stood and stared at the tree as the trail lights sparkled around the tree as if a firefly were buzzing circles around it. The sparkles stopped at the glittery star atop the tree. Loretta could only imagine how beautiful the lights would look at night, framed by the sparkling lights Pete had installed on the window.

Pete had been Loretta's handyman for the past couple of years. They'd met through his parents, who went to church with Loretta's family. Pete's father had been great friends with James and was concerned about Loretta living alone with no help. Since Pete had recently been released from prison after a five-year shoplifting bid and couldn't find a job, his father felt that Pete could gain some experience and earn some money while helping a church member who had recently lost her husband.

Loretta was apprehensive at first, but Pete turned out to be not only a great handyman, but he was great company. She was proud of him for his efforts in turning his life around. In the time he'd been out of jail, he'd finished his associate's degree, earned a certification in electricity, and had even gotten married and started a family. Over time, he'd become like a son to Loretta. There was nothing she wouldn't do for him. To Loretta, Pete was the perfect example of what a formerly incarcerated man could accomplish when given a chance to succeed.

"I'm kinda proud of myself," Loretta said, still smiling. She smiled as her eyes followed the chasing lights up the tree.

"You should be, Miss Loretta," Pete replied. "That's fire!"

"Now you see why I needed your help. It would have taken all day to install the wire, wrap the lights around it, and install the lights in the window. I might think I'm young, but I'm still an old lady."

"Now, Miss Loretta, old is only a state of mind. I done told you that."

"Go on with all that," Loretta said with a dismissive wave. "That sounds good in books and movies, but this is real life. I don't mind askin' for help when I need it."

"I hear you."

"So, what you doin' for Christmas?" Loretta asked, leading Pete to the kitchen. They sat at the breakfast bar.

"My Uncle Charles is coming in town so he's gonna be spendin' Christmas with my wife and me. My parents are coming by, too."

"Oh, that should be nice," Loretta said with a smile. "Where's he coming from?"

"He's visiting from Houston," Pete replied. He chuckled a little. "My momma calls him a forever bachelor. He got divorced about ten years ago and swore he would never get married again."

"I know that feelin'," Loretta said, slowly shaking her head. "When my James died a few years ago, I swore I would never get married again. I've been concentrating on me ever since, and I'm happy."

"I can tell you're happy," he agreed. "You're livin' in this big, beautiful house in Lakeview, you got a beautiful family, and you're livin' the retired life without a care in the world."

"Yes, God is good."

"All the time."

Loretta smiled and pointed at him. "And all the time?"

"God is good!"

They laughed at the old church phrase that was probably older than Pete, himself. Loretta believed every word of the phrase, but she couldn't help but laugh at the call and response of it all. Everyone knew what to say when they heard the words. Black people loved a good catchphrase, and she loved it.

"You funny, Miss Loretta, I tell ya," Pete said, wiping his eyes. "I wish my Uncle Charles saw life like you do."

"Whatcha mean, baby?" Loretta asked, scrunching her eyebrows in concern. "He depressed or something?"

"I wouldn't say he's depressed," Pete said. "Just jaded. Gettin' divorced in your sixties does somethin' to you. You're enjoyin' life. He's just mad at life."

"Oh, my," Loretta said with a frown. "I can't imagine."

"Yeah, my daddy is hopin' that spendin' some time with the happy part of the family will do him some good."

"I hope he's right," Loretta said, patting Pete's arm in support. "You want some coffee?"

Pete chuckled. "I'ma need somethin' a lil stronger than that. If you don't need nothin' else, I'ma roll on out and pick up one of them eggnog daiquiris from the Daiquiri Shop on the way home. The wife and I have some gifts to wrap while the boys are with their grandparents."

"You've got a good woman there, Pete," Loretta stated. "You two have a good thing goin' on. Your son and her son get along like brothers, and that's a blessing."

"You right," he agreed with a nod. "Those boys treat each other like blood. It's somethin' to see. And to this day, Tanya has never treated me like a convict. She makes me wanna be better."

"You're already better, son," she said, squeezing his hand. "And if I never told you before, I appreciate all you've done for me the last few years."

"Awww, it's my pleasure, Miss Loretta. Just make sure I get a bowl of that gumbo when you finish it."

"You know it."

Pete pumped his fist like he'd won the lottery. "Miss Loretta, if you ever decide to get married again, your cookin' is gonna make some man really happy."

Loretta laughed as they stood from their stools. She led him to the door, still smirking from the thought of ever getting married. "That was a cute sentiment, but Miss Loretta is too old to be looking for a boo."

"I hear you, Miss Loretta," he said with a chuckle. He opened the door and stepped outside, the rays from the setting sun highlighting his caramel-colored skin. "All I'm saying is you're a good lady. I appreciate you."

She smiled and pulled her handyman into a hug. "You're just full of the charm today, huh? Gotta love that holiday spirit."

"Just callin' it like I see it," Pete said as he released the hug. He skipped down the steps and waved as he stepped into his pickup truck.

Loretta waved as she watched him pull out of her driveway. Once he turned the corner, she backed into her home and again looked at her beautiful Christmas tree. It had gotten darker, so the sparkling white lights chasing each other in circles up the tree became even more enchanting. She opened her wine cabinet and reached for an open bottle of Malbec. After pouring herself a glass, she sat in her armchair to take in the Christmas magic a while longer. Cleaning shrimp and chopping seasoning could wait.

Her mind traveled back to the days when she and James cuddled in this same spot eight years ago, staring at their beautiful tree. There were no chasing lights and sparkles, but the Christmas spirit was there. Back then, there was no armchair. They only had a loveseat James had moved in to fill the room.

Loretta had still been trying to wrap her mind around moving into a four-bedroom home when it was just the two of them. Liza had been married almost ten years, so there was no chance she'd be moving back home. Sometimes Maya would spend the weekend or a couple weeks during her summer breaks, but that hardly constituted living in Lakeview. They were getting older, and she felt they needed to downsize.

"All your life you've been givin' and puttin' yourself last," James told her. "I want the last house you live in to be the home of your dreams."

And it was. It wasn't as large as the mansions down the street on the Lakefront, but it was beautiful, nonetheless. Hardwood floors, gourmet kitchen, natural lighting throughout the house, and a paradise oasis for a back yard. The best part was the house was walking distance from the lakefront, which made for beautiful scenery during their powerwalks. The house also wasn't far from the fairgrounds. She didn't care for horse races, but during Jazz Fest season, her home was prime territory for every family member who needed a parking space, a pre-game location, or an after party. Most would park at her house and catch a Lyft to the fairgrounds, which was much cheaper than paying for parking.

She and James began hosting their New Year's Eve parties about a year later. Having such a large home, they had quickly become the holiday destination for the family, so taking it a step further with a New Year's Eve party only made sense. Loretta loved it because it gave her even more reason to cook her favorite foods.

When James died a few years later, his insurance policy paid off the house, but it would be a while before the house would feel totally hers. Suddenly, she was by herself. She kept expecting James to shout her name, announcing he was home or beckoning her to watch whatever program he was watching. The silence was deafening.

For the first few months, she was almost afraid of being alone. Her powerwalks became longer in hopes of being so tired that she would fall asleep as soon as she returned home. She welcomed the company of Liza, David and Maya, and often let Maya spend weekends just so there would be more movement in the house.

The first New Year's Eve party after James's death almost didn't happen. No one thought Loretta would want to host a party so soon after losing her husband. But Loretta needed it. Having festive people in the house would keep her mind off the silence. Looking back, she was glad she never stopped hosting the parties. They kept her sane.

A buzz interrupted Loretta's trip down memory lane. She looked around and found her cell phone glowing across from her on her armchair's twin. She took a sip from her wine and then reached for the phone. The light from the screen lit up her face as she checked the text from her daughter.

Liza: *You finish your surprise?*
Loretta: *Yes, Ma'am, I did, and you're going to love it.*
Liza: *I better, the way you were being all mysterious.*
Loretta: *LOL! You'll see tomorrow.*
Liza: *What are you doing now?*
Loretta: *Drinking some wine. Going to be bed soon.*
Liza: *Already? It's not that late.*
Loretta: *I know. I'm tired. I'm just going to get an early start tomorrow.*
Liza: *I understand. We're going to watch a movie. We'll be by tomorrow after work. Love you!*
Loretta: *Love you, too. Have fun!*

Loretta took another sip of her wine and eyed the Christmas gifts she'd placed under the tree earlier that day. Soon, those boxes would be accompanied by even more beautifully wrapped gifts. In just a few days, Liza, David, and Maya would be gathered around her dining room table enjoying Christmas dinner. Later, they'd enjoy a football game while snacking on pound cake and eggnog. The neighbors would stop by to say hello, although she knew they were really coming to get some of her cake.

Her family had truly been blessed, and they owed it all to James. If only he could be here to enjoy those blessings with them.

Chapter 3

G irl, you are crazy!" Liza exclaimed as she laughed with her friend Sabrina. She laughed so hard she had to stop what she was doing and hold her chest.

"What's so funny?" Sabrina asked from Liza's speaker. "It's getting rough out here. I'm tired of only having a blanket to snuggle up to in the winter."

"I get it, but online dating?" Liza asked as she searched her cabinets and filled a shopping bag with groceries. With all the grocery shopping they'd done over the past couple of days, the cabinets in her tiny kitchen were overflowing. It was time to make some deliveries to Momma's house. "People are crazy these days. What if you meet a nut?"

"You have to take precautions. I never invite these people to my house. We always meet in a public place, and I'm very choosey about who I connect with."

"Still, I don't know. Have you met any nice guys?"

"Actually, I have. I'm going out to dinner with an attorney tonight. Divorced, no kids, and grew up Uptown. We went to the same high school, but he graduated a few years before me."

Liza raised her eyebrows in thought. He presented well, but … "What's wrong with him?"

"You are so cynical," Sabrina said, cackling in laughter. "I'll tell you what: I'll text you when I get to the date, during the date, and on my way home. Deal?"

"Deal," Liza agreed as she placed two cans of cranberry sauce into the shopping bag. "And send me a photo!"

"I can do that. If he doesn't agree to a selfie, it will be a red flag."

"Exactly, because what does he have to hide?"

"Right!"

"Where is he taking you?"

"Ruth's Chris."

"Nice choice for a blind date."

"Well, it kinda doesn't feel like a blind date. We've been communicating a while over text and FaceTime. We're even Facebook friends now. This is just the first time we're meeting in person."

"Nice. I hope it works out for you," Liza said, leaning against the counter. She reached for the sky and wiggled her fingers in a stretch, and then bent from side to side. "I'd better make a move. I told Momma we'd be coming by today."

"How is Miss Loretta?"

"She's good, still acting like she's forty instead of seventy."

Sabrina laughed. "She deserves it. She looks great for seventy."

"She does.

"Well, tell her I said hello, and I'm definitely stopping by to get my Christmas pound cake."

"I'll do that, but you can't bring your lil online boyfriend to my momma's house!"

The two women cackled in laughter as Maya walked into the kitchen.

"What's so funny?" she asked, grabbing an apple from the fruit bowl on the table.

"Sabrina's out here trollin' the Internet for dates," Liza said, wiping away a tear.

"Girl, don't be telling that child my business!" Sabrina snapped with mock indignation. "And ain't nobody trollin'!"

"Child?" Maya said, placing her hand on her hip. "I'm twenty. I am *grown.*"

Liza smirked and twisted her face at her daughter. "You're not grown yet."

"Tell her, Liza!" Sabrina cheered.

"Girl, lemme get off this phone," Liza said after a chuckle. "I'm trying to get to Momma's and back home before it gets too late."

"I understand," Sabrina said. "I'll see you on Christmas Day."

After ending the call, Liza dropped into a chair and tapped her chin in thought.

"What's up, Mom?" Maya asked. "You look like you're thinkin' about somethin'.

"Just thinkin' about Sabrina and her online dating situation. It just sounds crazy to me."

"I think it's pretty cool."

Liza gave her daughter a side-eye. "Of course, *you* would."

"No, seriously," Maya said, taking a seat across from her mother. "Lots of people are doing it now. Even some of my friends at school are meeting people online."

Liza scrunched her eyebrows and glared at her daughter. "Do *you*?"

Maya pursed her lips as if to say *get serious*. "No, Mom, I don't have a dating profile. Besides, I already have a boyfriend."

"Oh, yeah, that lil big-head boy Tyron."

"His name is *My*ron!"

Liza chuckled and waved her hand. "Whatever. You know your daddy doesn't like him."

"Daddy doesn't like anybody. Myron didn't even do anything wrong."

"Doesn't matter," Liza said, rising from the table. She opened the refrigerator and grabbed a bottle of water. "Where is your daddy, anyway?"

"Upstairs," Maya said, biting into her apple. "Now, back to the online thing. I've even seen sites for old people."

Liza stopped mid-sip. "Seriously?"

"Mom, you've obviously been married too long. You have no idea about the dating world."

"And a twenty-year-old sheltered girl who's never had a job does?"

"Yes, Ma'am! Who's the one on social media, AND who's the one a boyfriend?"

"Okay, dating guru, what are you gettin' at?"

Maya smiled as if she knew a secret no one else new. "What if Grams had a dating profile?"

Liza's eyes bucked as wide as saucers. "She has a dating profile? How do *you* know, and *I* don't?"

Maya laughed. "No, Grams doesn't have a dating site. At least I don't think she does."

Liza breathed a sigh of relief and leaned back in her chair, and then suddenly sprang forward again. "But what if we created her one?"

"Huh? Like in secret?"

"It would have to be. She refuses to get out and meet people."

Maya looked skeptical. "Weren't you just saying you thought online dating was crazy?"

"They are, but it would be nice to see what's out there. There may be some nice seniors who are just like Momma and don't get out the house. I'm sure older people aren't as crazy as younger people."

"What are you two conspiring about?" David asked as he walked into the kitchen."

"Mom wants to put Grams on dating site!" Maya reported.

"Way to ease into it," Liza snapped, kicking her daughter under the table.

"Ow!" Maya shouted, rubbing her shin.

"Don't abuse our daughter because she ratted you out," David said, folding his arms. "Now, what's this about a dating site?"

Liza's eyes darted everywhere in the kitchen except her husbands. "I—uh—just wondered—umm—what it would be like if Momma tried online dating."

"Does she *want* to date? Because last time I heard, she wasn't interested."

"She said she didn't want to go out and meet people," Liza protested. "This way, we would be doing the picking and vetting for her. All she would have to do is show up."

David shook his head and walked to the refrigerator as he rubbed his hands together. "I hope *we* means you and Maya, because I'm not in this one."

"What could go wrong?" Liza asked.

David turned back to his wife and stared at her. "Don't you know asking that question is a surefire prediction that something *will* go wrong? This thing could backfire."

"I don't think it'll be that bad," Liza said, her nose buried in her phone. "As long as she has a straight-forward profile and a few nice pictures, it should be okay. It's not like these people will have her phone number and address."

"That's not the point," David pushed.

"And the more I think about it, why not?" Liza added. "We could totally do this for Momma."

"Done!" Maya exclaimed, holding up her phone. Liza and David stopped debating mid-sentence.

Slowly and simultaneously, they turned toward Maya, who pointed her phone at them. She showed them a profile page with a photo of Loretta smiling and looking away from the camera. Liza recognized the photo from the night they went to see *Lion King* at the Saenger Theatre. Underneath the photo was a message that read:

I'm a retired high school teacher, devoted church member, a widow, mother of one and grandmother of one. I was married to a good man for over forty years, but since he passed five years ago, my daughter wants me to get back out there again. Whatever that means. I love cooking and taking care of my family. I'm looking for a grown man who still knows how to hold a conversation, dress for the occasion, and respect a woman who knows her worth.

"What do you think?" Maya asked proudly.

"What is happening here?" David asked, holding his head.

"I love it!" Liza exclaimed. "We're really doing this!"

"Your mother is gonna kill you," David warned Liza.

"It'll be harmless," Liza assured him. "A little curiosity couldn't hurt."

David chuckled and kissed her forehead. "Then do it. But be ready to run when she finds out."

"Dad, you're so doubtful," Maya said, looking back at her phone. "I'm going to tweak the bio some more and then start swiping."

"Well, thanks for setting up the profile, but I'm gonna need you to give me the username and password," Liza said.

"Why?"

"Because I don't trust your young self to do the pickin'. You'll mess around and pick a bunch of thirty-year-olds who look like Aaron Pierre."

"Wow, Mom. You don't know me at all."

"Oh, I definitely do, which is why you're gonna turn over that username and password."

David laughed and picked up the grocery bag that Liza had packed. He walked out of the kitchen, yelling back, "Tell me when y'all are ready to go. I'm about to load up the car."

Once he left, Liza warned, "Not a word about this to your grandmother."

"Why not? She has to find out sooner or later."

"I'd rather it be later. No need in getting killed before we find out whether this will be a bust."

* * *

The profile had already received twenty matches and five messages by the time David, Liza, and Maya pulled in front of Loretta's home. Liza was astounded. Some of the men were just as she'd feared—creepy. She silently deleted them without a thought.

A couple seemed nice but weren't attractive enough for her momma. Sorry, not sorry! Momma would already be mad at her for doing this. There was no need in making matters by setting her up with a booger bear!

Three men who left messages seemed to fit the bill. Attractive, friendly profiles, financially stable (or so they said), and normal-looking. Before she could really dig into their profiles, Maya's shout interrupted her.

"Mom! Look!"

Liza looked up to find a beautiful light display in Loretta's window. The sparkling lights seemed to call out to them.

"So, that was the surprise," David said. "She did that!"

"It's gorgeous," Liza agreed.

"I'ma get a closer look," Maya said as she opened the car door. She slammed it behind her and scampered up to the house, using her key to burst inside.

"I guess she's excited," Liza commented.

"And I know you are, too, but for a different reason," David replied. His eyes dropped to Liza's phone. "When are you going to tell her?"

"Not right now. Maybe after dinner. Maybe after I settle on a match."

"Don't put it off too long. This is a small city. You never know who she'll find out from. What if someone on the app recognizes her and mentions something?"

"Shoot," Liza said, biting her lip. "I didn't even think about that."

"You'd better tell her tonight."

"Okay, after dinner."

"Y'all comin' in?" Maya shouted from the doorway. "You've gotta see this tree!"

Liza answered with a half-smile and wave. Her short conversation with David had made her even more nervous. She knew in her heart she was doing the right thing, but would her mother understand that?

"Babe, let's get inside before that girl has the whole neighborhood staring at us," David suggested. Liza followed his gaze and caught a glimpse of the old man next door looking through his blinds.

"Mr. Leroy knows he can be a nosy somebody," Liza remarked with a giggle.

They exited the car and pulled the groceries and a few Christmas presents from the back seat. As they strolled up the sidewalk, Liza tried to make David promise not to say anything about the profile until she was ready.

"You know I'm not going to say anything, but I'm not the one you've gotta worry about," he said, tilting his head toward their daughter. "Who you need to be talkin' to is Mouth Almighty, Tongue Everlastin' in there."

Liza couldn't help but laugh at the 80s rap group Whodini reference, but her husband was right. She needed to get to Maya before she let anything slip. They were treading on very thin ice, and she couldn't risk falling too soon.

Chapter 4

You did *what*, Liza Renee?"

Liza looked around the dining room table, thankful Maya and David were there for backup. Turns out she didn't have to worry about Maya spilling the beans. Her daughter was mum about the entire situation, which drove Liza even more crazy. She couldn't even enjoy the surprise decorations for fear the secret would slip. By the time they sat down to dinner, she couldn't take it anymore and admitted to the deed.

"I – uh – we created a dating profile for you?" she stuttered before stuffing her mouth with mashed potatoes. She kept her eyes pointed at her plate to avoid what she was sure was her mother's glare.

David sipped his lemonade and looked away, determined not to be a part of the drama. Maya looked at her plate in a failed attempt to hide her smirk. Liza wondered how long her daughter would allow her to be on this hill by herself.

"Now, why would you do a crazy thing like that?" Loretta asked, dropping her fork onto her plate. She shook her head in exasperation.

"You didn't think there were good single men your age, and I – uh – *we* just wanted to show you there were some good ones out there," Liza said quickly. "And we didn't lie or anything. It's just your name, age, and a little about you."

Loretta held her head and rolled her eyes. "So now the whole Internet thinks I'm out here lookin' for a man?"

"Well, technically, just people in New Orleans," Maya said with a giggle.

"So, you're in on this, Maya?" Loretta asked, turning her disapproving gaze to her granddaughter.

"I kinda made the profile," Maya admitted, taking a sip from her lemonade.

Loretta looked at David. "You got anything to do with this foolishness?"

"Now, Momma Loretta, you know better than that," he said, shaking his head.

"Lord, have mercy," Loretta mumbled. "My family done gone crazy."

"It's not as bad as you think, Grams," Maya said. "People liked your profile. A *lot*."

"Well, of course they did," Loretta said without smiling. "I look good. But that's not the point. Now you're gonna have me wondering if every man I see has seen me on the Internet."

"Momma, it's not that bad," Liza said, pulling out her phone. She logged into the site and raised her eyebrows in surprise. "A few hours ago, you had about twenty matches and five messages. I personally went through and deleted the creepy ones or the ones not worth your time, but now you have one hundred and fifty matches and thirty-five messages. Momma, you're blowin' up!"

David suppressed a laugh and shook his head. Loretta, on the other hand, looked like she wanted to crawl under the table.

"One hundred and fifty matches?" she exclaimed. "LAWD, have mercy! What is this child tryin' to do to me?"

"Grams, chill a little!"

"Don't tell me to chill," Loretta snapped. "You and your momma got me out here lookin' like some desperate woman. What will my church members think?"

"I'll bet you some of them are on the site, too," Maya replied, laughing.

"That might be true of your lil college friends, but not people my age."

"Momma, older people need love, too," Liza said, "and just like you said the other day, people your age aren't gettin' out there looking for somebody. I'll bet there are lots of people your age who are good people and just haven't met anyone to spend time with."

Loretta grew quiet and closed her eyes. Liza wasn't sure if her mother would hug her or hit her. Either way, she braced for impact.

Loretta sighed. "Let me see this mess."

Liza smiled and slid her phone across the table, and Maya jumped up and ran behind her grandmother to help her navigate the site. Loretta slowly picked up the phone and squinted at the screen.

"I guess he's nice-looking," she said when she saw a photo of a silver-haired gentleman. His name and age appeared at the bottom of the photo. Frankie, sixty-eight. She frowned. "Uh! Too old to be wearin' an earring."

"If you don't like him, touch the screen and swipe left, and a new guy will come up," Maya explained.

Loretta did as she was told and was greeted with a new photo, which she swiped left just as quickly. The next photo was swiped even faster. She soon found herself in a swipe fest, unceremoniously dismissing fifteen men in less than thirty seconds.

"Grams, give me this phone!" Maya exclaimed, snatching it away from her. "You're not even givin' the men a chance!"

"That site is a waste of time," Loretta said, folding her arms.

"How would you know?" Liza protested. "You didn't even look at their profiles."

By this time, David was laughing so hard he had to leave the table.

"You're not helping," Liza called after him. She turned back to her mother and took the phone from Maya. "Momma, did you even look at the messages some of the men sent you?"

"Nope."

"Momma!"

Loretta huffed. "What do they say? I can't see them being much better."

Liza began scrolling through the messages in search of the ones she'd read earlier. "There was one gentleman I saw on there earlier who seemed pretty nice."

She slowed her scrolling and stopped on a grey-haired man wearing a fedora tilted to the side. He had a well-cut beard and an easy smile.

"Here he is. He's very attractive and guess what? He plays the saxophone."

Loretta widened her eyes, appalled. "I'm not going on a date with some saxophone player!"

"I thought you loved jazz music!"

"I love *Branford Marsalis*, not somebody who plays for tips on Frenchmen Street!"

"How do you know he plays on Frenchmen Street?" Maya asked.

"Baby, this is New Orleans," Loretta replied. "Saxophone players are a dime a dozen. And just about every band in this city plays on Frenchmen Street."

More masculine laughter came from the living room. Liza waved her hand toward him dismissively and continued trying to convince her mother to give Marcus a chance.

"Grams, what if he's cute?"

Loretta shot her a side-eye. "Y'all tryna kill me before I see seventy-one. One of these days you're gonna learn that when you get past a certain age, you need to have more to offer the world than just being cute!"

"You're a very beautiful lady, and I can tell you're very classy as well," Liza read. "I would love to meet you for drinks after my set at the Hotel Monteleone."

"He's inviting me to a hotel before he even gets to know me!" Loretta exclaimed. "Swipe left!"

"Momma!" Liza whined as Maya squealed in laughter. "He didn't invite you to a room. He performs there! Hardly Frenchmen Street. Now, you're just lookin' for a reason."

Loretta sighed and folded her arms. She looked down at her now-cold chicken and potatoes. "I'll think about it."

* * *

Loretta couldn't sleep that night. Part of her was still appalled by Liza and Maya's antics. How could they do something so public and embarrassing? Did they even consider how she'd feel about being placed in such a position?

She'd told them countless times she wasn't interested in dating. She was happy. Content. She was in an era where she was doing her own thing. Why couldn't Liza accept that?

But then again, another part of her was intrigued. Had that many men really found her attractive? She also had to admit the saxophone player seemed mildly interesting. The Hotel Monteleone was a beautiful luxury hotel located not too far from the French Quarter. It had a gorgeous rotating carousel bar. She and her sorority sister Mavis had gone there a few months ago after meeting for brunch at the nearby Harrah's Casino. If the saxophone player was performing there, he must be pretty good.

She paced from the kitchen to the living room, hoping to shake away her conflicting thoughts. What would James think about all this? She was sure he would think she'd lost her mind. Online dating? Swiping on strangers? She chuckled at the thought of him trying to understand it.

Her mind traveled back to his last days on this earth. Even knowing his time was short, his spirits were high. He'd even joked that she'd lose her beauty if she let the world pass her by. She didn't feel that way, but she had to admit that she could see why her family thought she had. In the five years since James had passed, she hadn't gone on one date. Not even a friendly outing to a Saints game.

Men had approached her in the past, but she always turned them down. There was never a good reason to do so if she was being honest. At first, it just felt strange being with someone besides James. After all, James had been her one and only for over forty years. That type of bond doesn't just go away overnight.

Over time, it got easier to be alone. Between cooking and exercising, she didn't care as much about dating. With James gone, she could focus on herself, and it felt great. She didn't have to work because James had left her a wonderful insurance settlement that paid off the house and left a nice chunk in the bank. They'd also purchased investment properties before he passed. One was used as an Airbnb, and she rented the other out to a single mother in the Lower Ninth Ward, which took care of the few bills she had left. She missed James, but she thanked God he had the foresight to make sure she would never have to work again.

"You were meant to shine. I hope you don't forget that, baby," he'd told her before he passed. And that was just what she did. She loved her life. Would dating disrupt that?

She walked back to the kitchen and pulled a carton of eggs and a box of unsalted butter from the refrigerator. She then walked into the pantry and returned to the counter with powdered sugar and flour. Maybe baking a pound cake would help her rest her mind.

Maybe Liza was right, she thought as she mixed the butter and sugar. Why *couldn't* she date while still living the life James had created for her? Maybe she had more living to do. No one said she had to remarry. But there was nothing wrong with having some company for a bit. Even if it started with the ridiculous idea of letting her daughter pick a man with a swipe.

She cracked an egg into the butter and sugar mixture and cut her eyes at her cell phone. She shook her head and cracked another egg.

"The devil is a lie," she mumbled as she turned on the mixer.

Finally, the feeling of curiosity overtook her. She turned off the mixture and looked up, shaking her head.

"Alright, James," she said, holding up her hands in surrender. "I'll try this once."

She picked up a dish towel and wiped her hands before snatching her phone from the counter. As she dialed Liza's number, she strolled to the wine cabinet. Once she heard her daughter's voice, she placed the phone on speaker and set it on a shelf in the cabinet.

"You good, Momma?"

"Oh, I'm great," Loretta said dryly as she poured a glass of Malbec.

"I'm sorry, Momma," Liza said quickly. "I'll delete the profile right now. Don't be—"

"Message the saxophone player and find out what time I'm supposed to meet him."

"Huh? Seriously?"

"Just do it before I change my mind."

Liza squealed in excitement, and Loretta could hear her tell David the news. He didn't share her enthusiasm. More like shock. Loretta snorted, expecting nothing else from David. She loved his stoicism.

"I'll message him now, and I'll make sure to chat with him a little more just to make sure he's on the up and up," Liza promised.

"Just give me the login information and I'll talk to him myself," Loretta said before taking a sip of her wine. She picked up the phone and carried it and her wine back to the kitchen. She felt some of the stress leave her body. Was that what giving up control felt like?

"You sure, Momma?"

"Just do it. But I'ma tell you now: If he asks me to split the bill or he even mentions playin' on Frenchmen Street, I'm blocking him *and* you!"

Chapter 5

I can't believe I let you talk me into this," Loretta grumbled as she looked at her reflection in her full-length mirror while Maya and Liza sat on her bed and watched.

As satisfied as she was with what she saw, she couldn't get past the fact that she was going through all this effort for a fedora-wearing saxophone player she'd never met before. She truly had better things to do on Christmas Eve!

"Stop, Grams," Maya interjected. "You look good. If nothing else, just go out and enjoy yourself. At least you're going to a nice place."

"What do you know about the Carousel Bar?" Liza asked, eying her daughter.

"I've seen it before. Tasha and I walked in there once to see the carousel. It's a cute spot. And no, we didn't get any drinks."

"Just makin' sure."

Maya shook her head. "These are the moments I wish I had gone to college out of state. Y'all just refuse to realize I'm grown."

"Grown folks live on their own and pay bills," Liza pointed out.

"Umm, ladies," Loretta cut in. "Can we get back to me for a little while?"

"Sorry, Momma," Liza apologized. "You look good, though. And Maya is right. Just have some fun tonight. No one is makin' you go steady.'

"Go steady?" Loretta asked with her nose wrinkled. "What are we, in the sixties?"

Maya and Liza giggled, and then Liza got up and hugged her mother. "Momma, I'm proud of you. I know this is a big step for you. Thank you for doing this."

Loretta smiled, starting to feel good about the night ahead. "You can thank me by cleanin' the shrimp and preppin' the gumbo ingredients tonight. Maya, I need you to chop up the seasoning and vegetables for the dressing and boil the eggs for the potato salad. This is Christmas Eve, and we have a lot to do before mornin'. This lil date is makin' me lose time so I'm gonna need you two to fill in the gap."

"We've got you," Liza assured her mother. "Just don't come back here all drunk in love."

"Oh, you funny," Loretta said, rolling her eyes. She pulled her phone from her purse.

"You confirming the time for your date?" Liza teased.

"No, I'm callin' a Lyft."

"Why? We could have driven you to the hotel."

"I don't want that man being privy to anything more than he needs to. He might mess around and see your license plate and try to track us down."

"You watch too many movies, Grams," Maya dismissed with a laugh.

"You need to be as careful as me," Loretta warned. "Y'all better stop thinkin' it can't happen to you."

"I hear you, Momma," Liza agreed as Maya nodded. "We're livin' in some dangerous times. Do what you have to do to feel comfortable."

"I'm glad you understand," Loretta said, putting her phone away. "My ride will be here in five minutes. Do I look alright?"

She spun around and fluffed her gray twisted out afro so her daughter and granddaughter could give her a final inspection. Choosing an outfit for tonight wasn't as easy as she thought it would be. She didn't want to wear jeans to the Hotel Monteleone, and wearing a dress seemed too churchy. She decided on a military green jumper Liza had given her last Christmas. It seemed casual enough while still looking dressy. Most women her age wouldn't dream of wearing such an outfit, but fashion had always been a passion of Loretta's. She may have felt old sometimes, but she never wanted to *look* old.

"You look good, Grams," Maya said, extra proud since she was the one who'd styled her grandmother's hair. "That Marcus guy won't even know what hit him."

"Oh, he'll know if he tries something," Loretta warned, pumping her fist like Muhammed Ali.

Liza laughed as she and Maya followed Loretta out of the room. She led them into the living room, where David sat watching Sportscenter. He looked up as they walked in and stood to his feet.

"Ladies and gentlemen, all hail the queen," he announced with a bow. Maya and Liza bowed as well, giggling when they saw the embarrassment in Loretta's face.

"Have fun tonight, Momma Loretta," David said. "We'll be here when you get back. And call us the minute something doesn't feel right."

"Yes, Sir," Loretta said, and then smiled. "I remember saying that same thing to Liza when she started dating. She chose well."

David smiled as Liza came over and hugged him. Before another word could be said, Loretta's phone buzzed as headlights shined through the window.

"Time to get out of here," Loretta announced. She pulled her coat from the closet and slipped it on. After pulling the straps tightly around her waist, she waved and then walked out. She closed and locked the door behind her, the cold air brushing across her face. She took a breath and whispered a little prayer as she walked to the car. "Here goes nothin'."

* * *

Loretta purposely showed up at the Hotel Monteleone early so she could catch the last few minutes of Marcus's set. The band had a good turnout, so it was easy to blend into the crowd. She wanted to be able to observe him without being noticed.

She recognized him right away. Marcus was a clean-cut brother with a silver beard who played his saxophone as if he were the only one in the room. Loretta had to admit he was pretty good. And true to his profile photo, he wore his fedora tilted to the side. It seemed to Loretta that the hat and his golden saxophone were like extensions of himself. She wondered if he wore that hat everywhere, or if it was part of his stage persona.

He was dressed nicely. His beige turtleneck sweater and copper-colored slacks gave him a casual youthful look. He looked healthy and seemed to love life. Loretta respected that. Hopefully he was a healthy eater and liked to exercise. But then again, she didn't plan on being around long enough to find out.

Loretta snaked her way through the crowd. As luck would have it, a couple left just as she reached the bar. She sat quickly, knowing everyone wanted to sit at the carousel.

"What can I get for you?" a female bartender asked. She had a friendly smile, but Loretta was sure she was exhausted. A full house on Christmas Eve couldn't be easy to handle.

"Do you have any good Malbecs?" Loretta asked.

"We sure do," the bartender affirmed. "Six- or nine-ounce pour?"

"Let's make it a nine. "I feel like I'm going to need it tonight?"

"Uh oh. Everything okay?"

Loretta looked around to make sure no one was listening and then leaned closer. The bartender followed suit as if she was about to hear a juicy secret. "I'm embarrassed to say my daughter set me up on a blind date. Can you imagine at my age?"

The bartender's smile grew even bigger. Loretta could see the cute dimples on her ivory skin. "I think it's great! You're never too old to find love."

"Now, you sound like my crazy granddaughter," Loretta said with a chuckle.

The bartender tapped the bar and smiled reassuringly. "Smart girl. I'll get that Malbec started for you."

"Ladies and gentlemen, this is gon' be our last for the night," the lead singer announced. Loretta turned toward the band to listen. "This one goes out to everybody. We wanna wish you all a Merry Christmas and a Happy New Year. This year ain't been easy, but we made it, y'all! And for all y'all visitin' the Big Easy for the holidays, enjoy your Christmas in New Orleans, 'cause ain't nothin' else like it!"

With that, the band broke into soulful version of Louis Armstrong's *Christmas in New Orleans* as the audience cheered and held their drinks in the air. The entire band swayed from side to side as the lead singer rendered an impressive rendition of the late Louie Armstrong. By the time Marcus broke in with his saxophone solo, Loretta found herself swaying along with the rest of the crowd. Dare she say she was actually enjoying herself?

As the song drew to an end, the lead singer announced, "That's gonna do it for us tonight, y'all. We're the Crescent City Brass Collective. If you like what ya heard tonight, bless the bucket, and please don't forget to tip ya bartenders!"

His last few words were nearly drowned out as the horn section blasted the end of the song and the band played out. Loretta smiled and turned back to the bar. She took a sip from her wine, hoping Marcus wouldn't take forever to find her. She felt she'd described herself well enough, and there weren't many women her age sitting at the bar. She'd give him fifteen minutes and then she'd call a Lyft and head home. No harm, no foul.

As she took another sip of her wine, a raspy voice came from behind. "Loretta?"

Her eyes widened and her throat suddenly went dry. The moment of truth had finally arrived. She turned around to see Marcus up close and in the flesh, standing there with his saxophone strapped to his back. He wore a leather jacket and a Burberry-style scarf. She was sure it was fake since she'd seen a street vendor on Canal Street selling the same scarves. Why was he wearing his coat anyway? Did he expect them to leave together? At least he smelled nice. Kind of a mixture of spice, tobacco, and leather.

"Yes, that would be me," she said without a smile, although she tried to look friendly.

Since the band was done, most of the crowd had begun filing out of the doors. A few patrons sitting at tables held their seats since the bar didn't close for another couple of hours and a new band would be setting up soon. Marcus laid his horn on the bar and sat on the stool next to Loretta. "Wow. You're even more beautiful in person."

She folded her arms across her chest and lifted one eyebrow. "I'm only here because my daughter tricked me into this."

Marcus froze and blinked. Then a smile spread across his face, and he laughed so hard that Loretta's cheeks hurt just watching him. She instantly grew embarrassed all over again.

"Well, I appreciate your honesty," he said, recovering from his laughter. He turned toward the bar and flagged down the bartender who had waited on Loretta earlier. "Hey, Misty, lemme get an Old Fashioned, and give my friend another of whatever she's drinkin'."

"Oh, so *you're* the blind date?" Misty asked, an amused smile plastered on her face.

Loretta gasped. "Maybe you can say it louder so the rest of the bar can hear you."

"I'm so sorry," Misty said, covering her mouth.

Marcus again burst into laughter as Misty rushed off to prepare the drinks. "I can already see I'm gonna like you. You a hard woman, Miss Loretta, but you ain't 'bout to scare me away," Marcus said, looking her up and down. The look didn't feel disrespectful, which put Loretta at ease. Maybe she'd give him twenty minutes.

"I enjoyed your band," she said, trying to break the ice. "Y'all are pretty good."

"I saw you dancin' to our last song."

"You did? Did you see me when I came in?"

"Nah, I just happened to look up during our last song and figured it was you."

"I guess there aren't too many old women sitting in here," Loretta said, looking around at the crowd.

"Woman, look at us," Marcus said with a smile. "Ain't nothin' old on us but our age."

She laughed and relaxed a little more. "You right about that."

They high-fived each other and then settled into conversation as Misty set their drinks in front of them. Loretta kept it surface level, telling him she grew up in the Tremé, had gotten married in her twenties, and widowed in her sixties. Marcus told stories of growing up in the Lower Ninth Ward, about how his father taught him to play music. He joined his first band when he was thirteen and had toured so much when he was younger that he never got married. It unnerved Loretta that a man could be in his late sixties and had never been married, but she guessed she understood. She'd met men before who'd placed career over marriage.

"I guess since you've never been married, you probably had a lot of girlfriends, huh?" Loretta asked leaning toward him.

"Who says I still don't have them?" Marcus asked, pumping his eyebrows and smiling.

Loretta gasped and sat back.

He chuckled. "See? Ask crazy questions, you get crazy answers."

"Okay, I'll give you that."

"You lookin' for a relationship?"

"I just met you."

"In general."

"I don't know."

Marcus smiled and folded his arms. "I don't think you are. Can I buy you another drink?"

"I'm not even finished with this one," Loretta said, holding up her half-full glass. "Besides, I can't stay too much longer. I still have Christmas dinner to cook. I can't be lettin' a man I barely know get me drunk."

"Yeah, maybe after I get to know you better," he replied with a laugh.

"Goodness, you're terrible!"

They laughed and talked more as she finished her wine. Eventually, she forgot about the profile, the app, and his possible harem of girlfriends. She even forgot to check her phone.

"You're disciplined," he said when she told him about her walking schedule.

"I buried a man at sixty-five because he wasn't."

Marcus nodded solemnly, his smile dimming just a little. "I hear that."

"Hey, Marc!" a male voice from the crowd called. Loretta and Marcus looked around, their eyes eventually falling on the drummer from the next band.

"What's good, man?" Marcus called out, sounding like a raspy thirty-year-old.

"Come gig with us," the drummer said. "Our sax player got family stuff goin' tonight."

Marcus looked at Loretta and then back at the drummer. "I gotta ask my lady friend first."

"Go on ahead," Loretta assured him. "I gotta get back to cookin'."

"You sure?" Marcus asked, even though he was already standing.

Loretta held back a laugh. He knew as well as she did that he was ready to cut this date short and get back to his saxophone. "Go ahead, Marcus. Have fun."

He smiled. "You gonna call me sometime?"

She smiled and held up her phone. "You know how to reach me.

"I certainly do," he replied. He gave her a hug and then backed into the crowd that had begun to form in front of the stage. The music started as soon as his feet touched the stage.

Loretta immediately recognized the shrill sound of Marcus's saxophone filling in the pockets of the music and watched in amusement as people cheered and began filming when he shimmied and gyrated as he played. He was nice and pretty fun. But he wasn't the one. She pulled up the Lyft app without another thought.

* * *

"Grams is home!" Maya announced before Loretta could even get the door open.

Liza scampered into the living room, her shirt covered in flour. "How did it go?"

"It went okay," Loretta said with a sigh. She dropped her purse on the sofa and kicked off her heels. The scent of fresh cornbread and collard greens greeted her nose as she walked into the kitchen. "Did you get all the ingredients for the gumbo prepped?'

"Yes, Ma'am," Liza said. "The shrimp is on ice, the sausage is sliced, the chicken is seasoned, and the trinity is chopped. Maya just put it all in the refrigerator. Before we leave, I'll put the shrimp shells in the crockpot so the stock will be ready in the morning."

Loretta nodded in approval. "And the turkey?"

"I seasoned and buttered it, and then put it at the bottom of the fridge," David reported from the kitchen doorway.

"And I see the greens are cooking and the cornbread is in the oven," Loretta said, glancing at the stove. "Y'all did good tonight. I guess I'll start on the dressing and the peppers before I go to bed."

"Ummm, you're not doing anything until you tell me about this date," Liza said, folding her arms.

"Yeah, Grams, you can't leave us hangin'," Maya agreed, mirroring her mother's stance.

Loretta's mouth dropped open, and she looked to David for help. He just chuckled and shrugged.

"Don't look at me," he said. "I said before I'm not in this."

"Momma, just tell us," Liza pleaded. "What was Marcus like?"

Loretta sighed and dropped into a chair at the kitchen table. "Let's just say he's in his sixties, going on twenty-five."

"Huh?" Maya asked, scrunching her face.

"She means he's still tryin' to live like he's in his player days," David explained, leaning on the counter.

"Exactly," Loretta agreed. "I'll admit the man has talent. He plays a mean sax. But the man dresses like the old man in the club with his fake Burberry scarf and that silly fedora. And he says he has a bunch of girlfriends!"

"Seriously?" Liza exclaimed.

"Wooooooooowwwwww," Maya said, lightly covering her mouth. "Did he really say that?"

"He had to be kidding. A man that age?" David wondered.

"Well, I wasn't gonna stick around to find out," Loretta said, shaking her head. She rose from the table and began stirring the collard greens. "His friends called him back to the stage to play with him and I got on outta there."

"Wow, Grams, did you even say bye?' Maya asked.

"Of course, I did. I'm not rude."

"Well, did you at least have a good time?" Liza asked, pulling the cornbread from the oven. She set it on the stove and began spreading a dollop of butter over the top.

"I will say it was good to get out and listen to some good music," Loretta said, lowering the fire under the greens. She reached for a plastic bag of green peppers and took them to the sink to wash them. "Maya, get the ground meat out of the fridge for me."

Maya did as she was told and set the package on the counter. She looked up quizzically. "But?"

"But I definitely won't be seeing the saxophone player again," Loretta confirmed.

"I can't blame you," Liza agreed. "You think you'll try again?"

"Who knows?" Loretta replied with a shrug. I'll think about it. Right now, the only thing I'm worried about is gettin' this dinner done in time for Christmas. You still got the mac and cheese?"

"Yes, Momma," Liza groaned. "The pan is in my fridge. We'll bring it over first thing in the mornin' so we can get it in the oven."

"Can't you bake it at your house?" Loretta asked. "I already got enough with the turkey and these peppers."

"She's got a point," David said. "We'll just get up a little earlier."

"That's fine," Liza agreed. "If that's the case, we'd better leave now. Tomorrow's gonna be a long day."

Maya yawned. "Fine with me. You need help with anything, Grams?"

"I'm fine," Loretta assured her. "Thank y'all for gettin' everything started for me."

"You're welcome, Momma," Liza replied, hugging her mother. "Merry Christmas."

"Merry Christmas to y'all," Loretta said, hugging her family. She followed them to the living room and watched as they filed out of the house. She then picked up her purse from the sofa and returned to the kitchen. Her phone buzzed just before she placed her purse on the table. She fished the phone from her purse and smirked when she saw a notification from the dating app. It was a message from Marcus.

Nice meeting you tonight. You deserve everything you're looking for.

"This man really thinks he's still young," Loretta mumbled with a laugh. Out of curiosity, she decided to look at a few more profiles, swiping left on most of them until she landed on a very distinguished looking gentleman. She looked at his profile and was impressed to see that he was a chef who owned his own restaurant. His name was Henri?

"Now, you know your name is Henry," she said with a laugh. Nothing about him looked French. Still, she was intrigued. She swiped right.

Chapter 6

"Merry Christmas!" Maya shouted as she and her parents walked into Loretta's home, greeted by R&B Christmas carols, the sparkling Douglas fir with dozens of gifts overflowing underneath, and the spicy scent of gumbo. They carried a medium-sized pan of mac and cheese and a large bowl of potato salad into the kitchen, where they found Loretta at the stove basting the turkey while singing along with the Temptations.

Loretta looked up and jumped when she saw her family standing in the kitchen, nearly knocking the turkey on the floor. "Y'all almost gave me a heart attack! When y'all get here?"

"I shouted Merry Christmas when I walked in," Maya said, placing the mac and cheese on the kitchen table.

"Yeah, Momma," Liza said, setting down the potato salad. "You in here blastin' music and can't even hear who's walkin' in ya house."

"That's real dangerous, Momma Loretta," David agreed with a smile.

"You know what? All y'all can leave!" Loretta snapped, drawing a roar of laughter from her family. She smiled and pulled them into a hug.

When she finally released them, Liza looked around the kitchen in awe. The stuffed bell peppers were perfectly done and sat on the stove next to the simmering gumbo and the pot of collard greens from the night before. The dressing had also been completed and sat proudly on the counter next to not only the pound cake Loretta had baked a couple nights ago, but two sweet potato pies as well.

"Wow, Momma," she said. "Did you any sleep at all last night?"

"I didn't have to do much," Loretta replied as she stirred the gumbo. She sprinkled a little gumbo filé across the top and stirred it in.

"Filé is what makes the gumbo *gumbo*," Liza remembered her mother explaining when she was a little girl. To this day, she wouldn't dream of making a gumbo without that magic seasoning.

"Y'all did most of the work while I was out on that so-called date," Loretta continued. She pointed to the coffeemaker just as her phone buzzed from the counter. "I made some coffee a lil while ago, David. You want some?"

"Yes, Ma'am!" David said, already reaching for the cabinet. As he reached for the mug, he and Liza shared a look when they noticed Loretta smile as she checked her phone. He shook his head, and Liza knew right away he was telling her to mind her business.

"Grams, you need any help with anything?" Maya asked. "I can wash the dishes for you."

"Thanks, baby, that would be helpful," Loretta replied. "Once you finish that, we can open the gifts and then get ready to eat."

"Sounds like a plan to me!" Liza exclaimed. "I've been dreaming about that gumbo!"

"And here I am thinking I was the one who put that smile on your face," David joked as he stirred his coffee.

"Eww! Daddy!" Maya scoffed. "Really?"

"You really have a talent for being inappropriate sometimes, don't you?" Loretta remarked with a slight laugh.

"What?" David asked with mock confusion. "That's not even what I meant."

"Sure, David," Liza said. "Forgive him, Momma."

"I always do," Loretta said. "So, son-in-law, are your parents stoppin' by this afternoon?"

"I don't know if I wanna tell you now," he replied. "You gonna tell on me?"

The family laughed again.

"Yeah, Grandma and Grandpa are stoppin' by around two," Maya said as she loaded the dishwasher. "I also asked Myron to come if that's okay."

"I get to meet ya lil boyfriend today?" Loretta asked. She clapped her hands. "This really is turnin' out to be a Christmas miracle!"

Her phone buzzed again, drawing curious stares from everyone. Again, David shot Liza and Maya a stern look, daring them to say anything. Maya immediately returned her attention to the dishwasher.

"My friend Mavis is comin' by for dessert," Loretta mentioned, not looking up from her phone.

"Yeah – um – and my friend Sabrina is also comin' over," Liza added.

"Oh, that's nice," Loretta said, finally putting down her phone. "She's my lil buddy."

"Yeah, you two have a few things in common," Liza remarked. David poked her in the side and again shot her a look. She looked up at him and gave him the same confused look he'd given them earlier.

* * *

"A Kamara jersey!" David exclaimed after opening Maya's gift. "Thanks, baby girl. You know that's my boy."

"Yep!" Maya said proudly. "You know I know nothin' about football, but I heard you mention his name a lot. Myron helped me pick out the jersey."

"Myron, huh?" David said, placing the jersey and its box on the coffee table. "He's a brave man for coming to meet the family for the first time on Christmas."

"I respect it," Loretta said, admiring her new designer purse gifted by her daughter. "It shows me that he's serious. I would think these young boys of today wouldn't celebrate a holiday with a girl they don't care about."

"Or he's a serious player with a lot of game," David remarked, leaning back on the sofa. "I'm reserving my judgment."

"David!" Liza exclaimed. "Stop it!'

"Yeah, Dad," Maya agreed. "He's a good guy. Give him a chance."

Loretta chuckled. "Reminds me of Cliff Huxtable from the Cosby Show. He didn't like any of his daughters' boyfriends."

"It's our job to protect our babies," David said proudly.

Before Loretta could respond, her phone buzzed again. She looked down and smiled when she saw another message from Henri.

Henri: *I hope you got some good gifts.*
She responded: *I absolutely did.*
Henri: *I'd love for you to come by the restaurant tonight so I can give you a gift, too.*
Loretta tilted her head and scrunched her face. *What gift?*
Henri: *I created a special dessert for Christmas, and it's been popular all day. I want you to try it.*
Loretta smiled. *I'll think about it.*

"Alright, I can't take it anymore," Liza exclaimed, commanding Loretta's attention. "You've been makin' googly eyes at that phone all day."

"Baby," David started, but then leaned back in his chair and pointed at her in surrender.

Loretta smiled and looked away, slightly embarrassed that she'd been caught.

"Did Marcus text you back or somethin'?" Liza asked, reaching for the phone.

Loretta snatched the phone from her reach and glared at her daughter. "Child, mind ya business!"

"Oops," Maya remarked, suppressing a giggle.

"I told you stay out of it," David said, shaking his head.

"Just askin'," Liza said as the doorbell rang.

"When I'm ready to tell you anything, you'll be the first to know," Loretta said as she rose from her chair. She waltzed to the door and peeked through the window. She smiled and announced, "David, baby, your parents are here."

He jumped up and greeted Johnny and Sylvia Lyttle as they marched in armed with a plastic shopping bag filled with gifts.

"Hey, old man," David said, taking the bag from his father. "Merry Christmas to you."

"I done told you 'bout that old man stuff," Johnny warned, putting his hands in a boxer stance. I can still take ya."

David laughed. "Not even on your best day."

"One of these days those two are gonna get tired of challengin' each other," Loretta told Sylvia with a smile.

Sylvia shook head, her copper-colored skin glowing from the sun rays shining through the window. "Not in this life."

"Hey, Grandma! Hey, Grandpa!" Maya greeted, walking toward them with her arms spread. They pulled her into a hug. "Merry Christmas!"

"Merry Christmas to you, my beautiful granddaughter," Sylvia replied. "David, pull those gifts out that bag. We brought a lil somethin' for everybody."

"What time we eatin'?" Johnny asked as David distributed the gifts.

"Well, ain't you impatient," Loretta said, walking into the kitchen. She returned to the living room holding with a stack of plates. Liza jumped up and helped set the table. "Everybody's not even her yet."

"Yeah, Grandpa," Maya added, "enjoy the moment."

"Damn, that," Johnny snapped, swatting away his granddaughter's words. "I'm hungry! I know you got some gumbo ready."

"Now, Pop Lyttle," Liza interjected, walking to the table with four wine glass stems between her fingers. She'd never been able to call anyone but James Daddy. Johnny didn't mind and had grown to like the name. Sylvia thought it was cute. "You know

Momma does these holiday dinners a certain way. No food will be eaten before it's time."

Johnny sighed, knowing he was fighting a losing battle. "Well, who all we waitin' on?"

As if on cue, the doorbell rang again.

"I'll get it," Maya said. "That's Myron. He just texted me."

"Girl, sit yourself down!" Sylvia ordered. "Don't you be runnin' to no doors for no man. He can wait."

Maya froze mid-step and returned to her seat, knowing better than to argue with her paternal grandmother. Loretta raised her eyebrows and smiled in admiration of her granddaughter's relationship with her other grandmother. Sylvia was a Southern woman to her heart and did her best to instill those values into Maya. Loretta was also a Southerner at heart, but her focus was more on Maya's studies and aspirations. To her, she and Sylvia made the perfect team. Between the two of them, Maya would turn out all right!

David walked to the door, opened it, and stared at Myron.

"Hey, Mr. Lyttle," Myron said tentatively. "Merry Christmas."

"Um hm," David replied.

"Let that boy in!" Loretta shouted. "David, you play too much."

"Way too much," Sylvia agreed.

The family laughed as the young man walked into the house holding a box and a small gift bag. He looked around nervously, but comfortable at the same time. "Merry Christmas, everyone."

"Merry Christmas, baby," Loretta replied. "I'm Maya's grandmother, Miss Loretta, and this is her other grandmother, Miss Sylvia."

"Nice to meet you both," he said, extending his hand.

"Boy, where you from?" Sylvia asked, scrunching her eyebrows. "You don't shake hands with two old ladies. You better hug us!"

Myron laughed and relaxed a little after hugging the two grandmothers. Maya came over and hugged his neck from behind.

"You know my parents already, and this is my grandfather," Maya said, pointing to Johnny with a Vanna White-style open palm.

"Good to meet you, young man," Johnny said, extending his hand. "I don't play that huggin' stuff."

Myron chuckled and shook his hand.

By the time Sabrina arrived, everyone was good and hungry. Loretta directed everyone to sit around the dining table as she, Liza, and Maya set the meal on the table. David then carried the turkey in on a serving tray, completing the holiday setting. After Johnny prayed over the meal, everyone dug in.

As they ate while laughing and making small talk, Loretta looked around the table and smiled. Only this time, the smile was slightly dimmer. She loved being around her family. They brought so much joy to her house each Christmas and New Year. Yet, this was the first year she felt a tinge of loneliness, and she couldn't understand why. All this time, she'd been perfectly content to be the only single person at her own party. But a couple days on a silly dating app had her wondering what it would be like to have a significant other sitting at her side.

She wondered what Henri was doing.

* * *

"Loretta, that turkey was on time," Johnny exclaimed, rubbing his round tummy. "And we not even gonna talk about that gumbo. Delicious!"

"Well, I'm certainly glad you enjoyed it," Loretta replied, smiling. She stood and began clearing the table, cuing the ladies at the table to do the same. The men, in turn, filed into the den to watch the game.

"Another successful Christmas dinner," Liza remarked, rinsing the plates and stacking them into the dishwasher.

"Yeah, we did our thing," Maya agreed with a smile.

"Oh, you helped cook?" Sylvia asked with genuine shock. "Whatcha cook, baby?"

"Yeah, baby," Liza added with a smirk. "Whatcha cook?"

As if sensing what was about to come, all the women stopped and looked at Maya, smiles tugging at the corners of their mouths. Maya looked at all of them and folded her arms. "Look, I didn't have to cook. I was a valued assistant."

The women cackled in laughter. Sabrina rubbed Maya's shoulder in consolation. "That's alright, Maya. I didn't learn how to cook until I graduated from college."

"She ain't lyin'," Liza agreed. "She was at our house every weekend."

"I had to be," Sabrina said. "I was juggling a double major and a job. Ain't nobody had time for cookin'."

"Well, I didn't mind cookin' for you," Loretta said, thinking back to the days when Liza and Sabrina sat in the den doing their homework and watching old episodes of Def Comedy Jam. The girls were inseparable. Since Loretta and James had never had any other children, she worried about Liza being lonely, but once Sabrina came along, she quickly became like a second daughter.

"I'm glad to hear that since I was over so much," Sabrina said with a smile. "I think Mr. James was tired of seeing me so much."

Loretta chuckled. "He didn't mind. If you weren't interrupting his sports, he didn't have a problem."

A roaring cheer came from the den. Sylvia laughed. "These men and their sports."

"I might go in there and join the men in a minute," Sabrina said.

"Yeah, me too," Maya agreed.

"Since when did you start likin' sports?" Liza asked, shooting her daughter a quizzical look.

"Since that lil boy came over," Loretta replied for her, drawing laughs from the other ladies. She smiled at her granddaughter and pat her on the back. "I don't blame you. He's nice-looking. He better be treatin' you right."

Maya beamed. "He is, Grams. He's part of the reason I'm getting an A in Genetics."

Liza and Loretta smiled and exchanged an impressed glance.

"Cute *and* smart? Not a bad combination," Sylvia remarked.

"Just don't lose yourself," Loretta said. "I remember those days of gettin' so wrapped up in my boyfriend that I forgot I needed to have a life of my own."

Sabrina nodded in agreement. "Yeah, that happened to me, too. Probably one of the reasons I'm not married."

"I think we all go through it at least once or twice," Liza added as she pulled the orange juice and an open bottle of champagne from the refrigerator. She looked thoughtful as she poured her mimosa. More champagne than juice, of course. "Remember my friend Brittany, Sabrina?"

"Vaguely," Sabrina replied.

"You remember—short, light-skinned girl? She was a cheerleader."

Sabrina cocked her head in thought. "Yeah, I think I remember her."

"That girl didn't have friends her first two years of college," Liza said. "She was always hanging under that boy she was dating. Never had time to hang with us. That's probably why you don't remember her."

"That's sad," Sylvia said. "I still see some of these young girls around my house actin' like they can't make a move without askin' for a boy's permission."

"It's not like that with me and Myron," Maya assured her paternal grandmother. "I still hang with my friends. I promise I have a life outside of my boyfriend."

"I'm glad to hear that, baby," Sylvia said, patting Maya's hand.

"I can vouch for that," Liza said. "If I recognized a problem, I woulda stepped in a long time ago."

Loretta rested her elbows on breakfast bar, enchanted by the conversation. Three generations of wisdom had clashed in her kitchen, and it was a sight to see, whether she agreed with everyone's views or not.

Her phone buzzed again just as the men erupted in cheers, probably from a touchdown or something. She slipped her hand into her pocket and pulled out her phone. A new message notification from Henri.

Henri: *You enjoying the family?*

She smiled and typed, *Yes. We're having a great time. I have a houseful.*

Henri: *I'm jealous. I'm over here working like a dog. You'd be surprised how many people go out to eat for Christmas.*

Loretta glanced up, hoping no one was watching her this time. *I can imagine.*

Henri: *You mind if I take a raincheck until tomorrow? Maybe I can take you to brunch.*

His question brought a sigh of relief. She really had no idea how she would get all these people out of her house at a decent hour. And truth be told, she didn't she want to rush them out. She was genuinely enjoying the company. *That'll work. Let me know where we should meet.*

"More secret messages?" Liza whispered from behind.

Loretta jumped, dropping her phone. "What I tell you about being nosy?

Liza giggled. "I don't know why you're trying to hide it. You're starting to enjoy this online thing."

"I don't know what you're talkin' about, Liza Renee," Loretta protested, trying her best not to attract even more attention. "But I do know you better not spread my business. I don't need anyone else knowing about this."

"It's nothin' to be ashamed of, Momma. Heck, Sabrina's online dating, too."

Loretta looked at her daughter and then over to Sabrina, who was pouring her own mimosa while laughing with Sylvia and Maya. "Are you serious?"

"Yes! She's how I got the idea to make your profile."

"Sabrina put you up to this?"

Liza laughed quietly, her shoulders shaking in animated joy. "No, Momma. She told me she was on a dating app. I thought she was crazy, but the more I thought about it, the more I thought this would be good for you. I mean, it seems to be workin'. You're over here smilin' like a schoolgirl."

Loretta dismissed her daughter's words with a quick wave. "Girl, ain't nobody actin' like no schoolgirl."

"There's nothin' wrong with being happy, Momma. Have some fun."

Loretta smiled slightly. "I do have to admit it's nice being flirted with. Marcus wasn't for me, but what was nice was that the first thing he did was tell me I'm beautiful. That was nice to hear."

"Love that! Is that him who's been messaging you?"

"Nope."

"Then who?"

"A chef named Henry. Well, he calls himself Henri, but I don't think that's his real name."

Liza smiled and raised her eyebrows. "Okay, Momma. Look at you makin' a roster!"

"One message from one man is hardly a roster."

"If this is a new man messaging you after you went out on a date last night, I would say you're buildin' a roster."

Loretta scrunched her nose. "Shush, child."

Chapter 7

Loretta woke up the next morning with expectation. She was surprised at how much lighter she felt after opening up with Liza about online dating. It didn't feel as much like a dirty secret. She still wasn't sure if she wanted to tell the whole family, but the more she thought about it, why did they even need to know? It was her business.

She got out of bed and bent down, stretching her hands between her legs and touching the floor behind her. She hovered there for a few second longer, enjoying the stretch she felt in her lower back. It was still early, so she decided to take a walk on the lakefront before meeting Henri. She slipped on a pink warmup suit, grabbed her keys, and headed out.

"Habari gani, Mr. Leroy!" she greeted when she saw her neighbor sitting on his porch. He had the same angry look he always had, but Loretta had grown used to it after twenty years of living next to him.

He looked at her curiously. "Habara *what*?"

"Habari gani," Loretta repeated. "It's Swahili for *what's happening* or *what's the news*? Today's the first day of Kwanzaa. Umoja."

Mr. Leroy pursed his lips into a tight line and shook his head. "I don't participate in all that. Too much to be rememberin' at my old age."

"Now, Mr. Leroy, you're not that much older than I am," she replied, marching in place to increase her heart rate. "You need to be out here walkin' with me. Exercise would probably do that old body some good."

"Awww, go on with all dat," Leroy dismissed. "I'm good right where I'm at."

Loretta chuckled and began her walk, calling back him, "If you say so."

The cool air felt crisp as it brushed past her face. New Orleans winters felt more like autumn in other cities. Today, it was around sixty degrees. Some New Orleanians thought that was freezing weather, but for Loretta, it was the perfect walking weather.

She sped up her pace slightly and began pumping her arms. Eventually, the lakefront showed up on the horizon. A couple of fishermen sat on the shore steps, probably only fishing for fun. She couldn't imagine her seafood dinners coming from so close to shore. Or if they did, she'd rather not know about it.

She continued walking, passing a young man sitting on the hood of his car. He looked sad as he stared at the water. Loretta's heart went out to him, wondering whether he'd spent the holiday with his family, or if he had nowhere to go.

The Willis family was blessed. They'd had a house full of people, a tree loaded with gifts, and a table loaded with food. Loretta's refrigerator had so many leftovers, she could host anther family dinner if she wanted to. It was easy to forget there were people in her city who didn't have it like they did. She made a note to herself to pack up those leftovers and take them to the one of the shelters when she got back from her brunch date.

Brunch date. She still couldn't believe those words were even in her thoughts. If someone had told her she'd be meeting a man she'd found on the Internet, she'd have sworn they were crazy. Heck, just last week she would have never even fathomed such a thought.

By the time James had passed, online dating was totally foreign to them. Being married forty years, they had no need for such technology. But she could now see the convenience of it. She could secretly vet hundreds of men without ever leaving the house. She could be as judgmental as she wanted to without being seen as rude. She could converse with several men at once without appearing to be "playing the field." It was interesting.

She slowed her pace and pulled out her phone. After opening the app, she found four new messages.

Marcus: *I hope you enjoyed your Christmas. When can I see you again?*

Henri: *Last night was killer! These tourists are a trip. Looking forward to brunch.*

Jimmy: *Hey beautiful. How was your Christmas?*

Trevor: *I would love to make love to you. Can you send me a full-length picture?*

That last message nearly made her drop her phone. Some men just didn't grow out of being crass and inappropriate. Was she supposed to think it was cute that a man she'd never met and was messaging her for the first time was already trying to get her into bed? The nerve!

She stared at the message and noticed a block function. After putting the function to use, she responded to Henri, ignoring Jimmy, whom she didn't know, and Marcus, whom she didn't plan to see again. *I'll see you at noon.*

* * *

Loretta stepped out of her Lyft and looked around for the restaurant. She suddenly felt a wave of nervousness as she caught a glimpse of her reflection in a storefront window. Today's outfit was a slightly lowcut blouse with a fitted pair of jeans and low heels. Had she done too much or too little? She prayed this man wouldn't take one look at her and assume she was trying too hard to look young. Didn't she secretly judge Marcus for doing the same thing?

The restaurant was located on Magazine Street in the city's Lower Garden District, a picturesque historic area full of grand homes, antique shops, coffee shops, restaurants, and bars. Due to segregation, Loretta never dared to go into the area as a child. The late fifties and early sixties were not the best times for young Black kids to be running around Uptown. There weren't signs in the windows, but it always remained cleared that outsiders—especially of the darker hue—weren't welcome.

Loretta was well into adulthood before she felt comfortable enough to venture onto Magazine Street. James had fearlessly taken her there on their first date. She was glad she went. Over the years, the Lower Garden District became more racially diverse with middle class, working residents living among the wealthier people who chose not to move. The vibes had remained affluent, but in a more relaxed sense. The restaurants weren't overly crowded, and the shops had expanded to include organic grocery stores and other local businesses. This was the area Loretta encouraged visitors to visit. The French Quarter was great, but the Garden District had a different appeal.

Henri was easy to recognize. Since it was the day after Christmas and still late morning, the restaurant was slightly empty. Henri was the only person sitting at the bar, and he looked almost exactly like his photo. He sat quietly scrolling on his phone as he sipped from a Bloody Mary. Loretta hated those things. Tasted like cold tomato sauce.

"Henri?" Loretta whispered as she walked up behind him. She lightly touched his back to get his attention.

He turned around and smiled as he locked eyes with Loretta. She held her breath, wondering if his first words would come out with a French or Creole accent.

"What's up, baybay," he greeted, welcoming her into a hug. Definitely wasn't a French accent. It was very New Orleans.

Loretta smiled and returned the hug. As she sat down, she couldn't help herself. "I was expecting a French accent."

He laughed and took another sip from his drink before waving the bartender over. He lifted his drink toward Loretta. "You want one?"

"Um, no, I'll just take a Malbec," she replied.

The bartender nodded and walked away. He returned a minute later with a glass of red wine. Loretta nodded in thanks and then took a sip.

"So why you thought I was French?" Henri asked once the bartender walked off.

"Your name is *Awn-ri*, right? Sounds French to me," she replied, looking confused.

"The marketing worked!" he exclaimed with a belly laugh. A couple looked up from the table next to them. He noticed and turned down the volume a bit, maintaining his smile. "My name is Henry, with the American pronunciation, but my mom was pure Creole and thought it would be better to spell it the traditional French way."

"But why not just pronounce it the French way?"

"Because she knew Black folks were gonna say it wrong anyway."

They chuckled together.

"That's too funny," Loretta said.

"What's even funnier is when I opened my restaurant, I started gettin' all these white tourists visitin' my spot. I guess my name sounds fancy—Chef *Awn-ri* DePaul. I just went ahead rolled with it."

They chuckled again.

"You wanna stay here, or do you wanna get a table?" Henri offered, stirring the rest of his drink with his straw.

"A table sounds good. That way I can look you in the eyes."

They laughed again as they snagged a table next to the couple who'd stared at them earlier. A waiter who was dressed like a skateboarder in cargo shorts and a T-shirt took their orders once they settled into their seats and then quickly walked off.

Without even trying, they'd broken the ice and had fallen into an easy getting-to-know-you conversation that felt comfortable and familiar. Loretta once again went through her spiel of being a widow, retired teacher, and mother of one. Henri, on the other hand, had a marriage that ended after six years, but he had three sons, ages thirty, twenty-five, and sixteen. They helped run his restaurant, which was located near City Park.

"Your youngest child is younger than my granddaughter," Loretta couldn't help but point out. She shifted in her seat.

"Yeah, he came as a surprise," Henri admitted. "I was dating a lot of younger women, but by the time his mother came along, I thought I was done havin' kids."

Loretta raised her eyebrows, fighting the urge to inform him that condoms do more than prevent pregnancy. Instead, she changed the subject.

"So, what kind of food do you serve at your restaurant?" she asked, tracing the top of her wine glass with her pointer finger, glad he couldn't see her knee bouncing impatiently.

He smiled. "I like to say it's elevated Creole cuisine with a twist."

"A twist, huh?"

"I add a little drama to every dish," he explained. "Kinda like fusion, but I take traditional dishes and give them a modern take. I serve three kinds of gumbo. I have a traditional Creole recipe with tomatoes, a seafood gumbo with crabs, lobster, shrimp, and crawfish, and I also have an elevated vegan gumbo that's outta this world."

"Vegan gumbo?" Loretta asked with a frown. "I like to eat healthy, but some things don't hardly need to be vegan, and gumbo is one of them."

"I'll bet when you taste it you're gonna change ya mind," Henri said as the waiter set their food and another round of drinks in front of them.

Loretta picked up her knife and fork and began slicing her salad to make her lettuce bites smaller. "I don't think so. The only thing I like vegan is right in front of me, and even then, there better be some chicken on it."

He smiled, undeterred. "You gonna see, Miss Loretta. You should let me give you a vegan cookin' class one of these days. I'll bet you won't even taste the difference."

"I don't know about that."

"You'll see. I'm surprised you're not vegan anyway. You look great."

"I'm a New Orleans girl to my heart," Loretta said after swallowing a forkful of salad. "I love to cook, and I love to eat. And because I love to cook and I love to eat, I exercise three times a week, skip the junk food, drink lots of water, and I save the heavy food for the holidays."

"Well, go 'head on!" Henri cheered with a clap. "So, who taught you how to cook?"

"My momma, of course," she replied. "Momma used to tell me I needed to know how to cook because I don't care how beautiful you are, you can't keep a man on just your looks. Beauty fades. I guess after over forty years of marriage that ended in 'til death do us part, she must have been right."

Henri smiled and leaned in closer. "It's nice talkin' with a woman on my level. You make me wish I had gotten married again."

"Maybe if you didn't just date those young girls, you probably could have," Loretta said before she could stop herself.

Henri clapped his hand over his heart. "That one hurt, right there."

"I'm sorry," she said, taking a sip from her wine. "I'm all up in your business."

"No, it's all right. I ain't got nothin' to hide."

She nodded, encouraging him to keep talking.

"My wife was the mother of my first two boys," Henri explained. "We divorced after my second son was born."

"Why, if you don't mind me asking?"

"It was my fault. She was goin' through that postpartum depression stuff, but at the time, I thought it was me she had the problem with," he explained. "He took a big swallow of his bloody Mary and glanced momentarily out of the window. "The more she would get mad with me, the more time I started spendin' out the house. Pretty soon, I moved out completely and she filed for divorce."

"Sad," Loretta commented. "Sounds like you were both goin' through some things."

"You ain't lyin'. She was gettin' used to bein' a stay-at-home momma of two small kids, and I was out there chasin' restaurant dreams. I had to learn the hard way that just because she didn't have a career didn't mean she wasn't under her own type of pressure."

Loretta's knee-bouncing slowed to a stop. She lifted her wine as if toasting him, and said, "Congratulations. You been workin' on yourself."

"Absolutely have," he replied, lifting his glass in return. "And believe it or not, I would like to get married again. Soon as I meet the right one."

His eyes locked with hers, and her knee again began bouncing. *You're ready to be married, but you're dating young girls? How does that make sense?* She surmised that she didn't fit what he was looking for. But why did he ask her out?

"I have to admit I don't know where or how I fit into your plan," Loretta sad, pushing away her empty plate and folding her hands in front of her.

"How you mean?" he asked, propping his cheek in the palm of his hand. His animated eyes never left her questioning eyes.

"You said earlier that you're used to datin' younger women," she stated. "I'm seventy, way older than the women you usually date."

"True, but I need somethin' different in my life. These young girls aren't doin' it for me anymore."

"Doin' what?"

"Challengin' me. Havin' real conversations. Havin' fun that doesn't involve TikTok and hookah. I'm gettin' old, Loretta. I can't be out here runnin' like a young buck no more."

Loretta smirked and leaned back in her chair. "You funny. So let me get this straight: You gave all your energy to women your sons' age, and now that you're tired, you wanna slow down with a woman *my* age?"

Henri blinked, taken aback. "You got me all wrong, Loretta."

She leaned forward. "I might be seventy, Henri, but I'm not a consolation prize. And I sure not lookin' to sit on the porch and wait to die."

Henri raised his hands in mock surrender. "Whoa, now. I didn't mean it like that."

"So, what did you mean??"

He sighed. "Look, maybe I didn't explain it right. What I'm sayin' is, I'm tired of women who only want a good meal and to go viral. My restaurant is nice. Really nice. My name has been gettin' out there so you let some of these girls tell it, I'm a means to a come up. I guess I got caught up in that. But for the last couple of years, I've been slowin' down, lookin' for somebody with depth."

He smiled. "You could be the one if you stop bein' so mean to me."

Loretta tilted her head and smirked again. "Is that supposed to be your way of flatterin' me?"

Henri smiled and relaxed a little. "Maybe a little. But I mean it."

She gave him a long, measured look but she didn't soften completely.

"I had a good time today," she said, "and I'd love to go out again someday, but I need you to understand that I'm not your last resort. I don't want you thinkin' I'm just gonna settle for the first man who blinks my way."

Henri's smile grew wider. "I'm sure I'm not the first man to blink your way. You're too beautiful."

"You're just full of charm, aren't you?"

"Am I wearin' you down?"

"We'll see."

Henri was exhausting, but Loretta had to admit he was also genuine. She may not have liked everything he said, but she gave him credit for telling the truth. Why not hang out with Chef Playboy? She wasn't going to grow old with him. She was already old. And he definitely wasn't the one. James would turn over in his grave if she thought any differently. Maybe he would be someone fun to talk with from time to time until she found Mr. Right. She might even take his vegan cooking class one day.

* * *

That night, Loretta called Liza and gave her a full report.

"He's a character, but I'm not here for raising kids," Loretta said, kicking off her heels. Without undressing, she lay across her bed and wrapped herself in her throw blanket.

"Kids? What do you mean? He's childish?" Liza asked.

"Pretty much. He has a sixteen-year-old son!"

"What? How old is this man?"

"Only a couple years younger than me. He has two other grown sons, but he said the sixteen-year-old came as a surprise."

"Lord, help! You've gotta be kiddin' me."

"I wish I was," Loretta replied with a laugh. "And get this!"

"It gets worse?"

"He said he's used to dating young women, but he's ready to settle down with someone his own age."

"Oh, so you're the little old lady he's settlin' for?"

"I guess so."

"How demure."

They cackled in laughter like two old friends.

"Well, what did you do the rest of the day, because I know you got away from that man as soon as you could," Liza commented once she recovered from her laughter.

"Actually, I met up with Mavis and we walked around Magazine Street and stopped in some antique shops," Loretta said. "You shoulda heard how she howled when I told her about Henri."

"I know she acted a fool," Liza said, a smile in her voice. "Did she say why she didn't make it to Christmas dinner yesterday? I thought she was comin' for dessert."

"Yeah, she apologized. She got double-booked."

"Sounds about right. I'm surprised you told her about your online dating debacles. I thought you didn't want anyone to know."

"I didn't, but the more I thought about it, I don't care. The people who matter won't care, and most likely the people who care won't matter."

"I like that," Liza replied. "Momma, I know this is a big step for you, and you're handling it like a true queen."

"Well, thank you, daughter. You and Maya pushed me into this, but I'm glad you did. But right now, I'm gonna run. I wanna pack up those leftovers and drop them off to that women's shelter Uptown."

"Aww that's nice," Liza replied. "Just don't give away the gumbo. David and I have plans for that."

Loretta laughed. "No problem. I'll leave it in the fridge."

She ended the call and lay on her back, staring at the ceiling. This was actually happening. After five years of concentrating on just herself, she was back in the dating world.

Chapter 8

Habari gani, Vashawn," Loretta greeted the next morning as she sat up in bed. Her cell phone had awakened her from a good dream, but she tried to make it a habit to always sound cheerful when her tenants called. *Why sound grumpy when people are paying you?*

"Habari gani to you, Miss Loretta," Vashawn replied. Loretta smiled, grateful that someone returned the greeting. Although she didn't know a lot about Kwanzaa, she loved what it stood for. It was Day 2—Kujichagulia, which meant self-determination, a great way to describe Loretta's new state of mind.

"I'm so sorry to be botherin' you so soon after Christmas Day," Vashawn said, "but our heating vent been rattlin' super loud. It woke up my baby last night."

"Oh, baby, I'm sorry to hear that," Loretta said, rising from her bed. "How long has this been goin' on?"

"Since the day before Christmas. I was tryin' not to bother you during the holiday."

"That's too long. That baby needs his rest, and you do, too. You still workin' that waitress job?"

"Yes, Ma'am," Vashawn replied, "but I'm hopin' to move to somethin' better soon."

"Well, I hope your boyfriend is still helpin' you in the meantime," Loretta said, rolling her eyes.

"He is."

"Good. Lemme call Pete and we'll try to swing by later this mornin'."

"Thank you, Miss Loretta. I'll see you soon, I hope you enjoyed your Christmas."

"I certainly did," Loretta said as she stepped out of bed. "I'ma see you later."

A heating vent? Vashawn's boyfriend certainly could have taken care of that instead of making her bother Pete during the holidays. She knew he would come, but she hated to bother him, especially since he had family visiting.

She dialed his number as she walked to the bathroom and listened to the rings, fully expecting him not to answer. To her surprise, he picked up on the third ring.

"Hey, Miss Loretta," he greeted. "Belated Merry Christmas!"

"Habari gani, Pete," she replied. "Are you busy today?"

"Me, my daddy, and Uncle Charles were just runnin' errands. Whatcha got goin' on?"

"My tenant in the Lower Ninth Ward called me about a rattlin' vent. I'm sure her boyfriend could probably fix it himself, but that boy ain't really good for nothin'. Can you meet me over there?"

She heard him groan under his breath, but she knew he was too polite to refuse her.

"I can go over there, but it won't be until later," he said. "I still got Dad and Uncle Charles with me."

"Hey, Sister Willis," she heard Pete's dad call out.

She smiled. "Tell Brother Randall I said hey."

She then heard moving around and muffled voices. After a few seconds, she could hear Pete's voice clearly.

"Miss Loretta, we can go ahead and meet you now. You mind if Dad and Uncle Charles tag along with me?"

"No, I don't mind. It'll be nice to meet your uncle. Where y'all at now?"

"We're 'cross the river," Pete said. "We should be there in about forty-five minutes to an hour. Can you text me the address?"

* * *

The house was located on Tennessee Street, one of the streets most affected by Hurricane Katrina in 2005. The house was only a couple of blocks from the levee. Most people thought she was crazy for buying a duplex so close to the levee wall, but she and James had gotten it for a great price. And with James being a construction worker, the repairs cost next to nothing.

Between Pete and Loretta and the government grants she received for rebuilding in the Lower Nine, the home was kept in pristine condition. As long as their tenants did their part and kept it clean, the rental was a cash cow that she had to worry very little about.

James had painted the house white with a cool sage green trim. They then rented the house through Section 8, a federal rental assistance program designed to help low-income families live in suitable housing. Their tenants paid next to nothing to rent because the government paid Loretta directly. Different families had rented the home over the years, but she had a special affinity for Vashawn, who'd moved in just before Thanksgiving 2023.

Vashawn was a twenty-four-year-old single mother of an eight-year-girl and a six-month-old boy. On paper, she lived in the home alone with her children, but Loretta was wise enough to know Vashawn's boyfriend was living there on the low. Loretta would have reported him, but she couldn't risk Vashawn and her kids being put on the street.

She pulled in front of the house just as Pete's truck rolled up behind her. Pete hopped out with his usual smile, toolbox in hand. The passenger door then swung open, and out stepped Pete's dad and a tall, honey-colored man with short salt-and-pepper curly hair. He was dressed in a clean black sweater, dark jeans, and gator-skinned cowboy boots. Definitely not an outfit you wear to do manual labor. *So, this is Uncle Charles.*

"Merry Christmas, Sister Willis," Pete's dad Donovan greeted, giving her a friendly hug. "It's good to see you."

"Likewise, Brother Randall," Loretta replied. "How's Sister Randall?"

"Doin' good, doin' good," he replied. He then swung his hand toward Uncle Charles. "Lemme introduce you to my brother Charles."

Loretta looked his way and gave him a friendly smile. Charles responded with a half-smile and piercing eyes that immediately made her feel uncomfortable. Maybe it wasn't such a good idea to let Pete bring his family. Hopefully Uncle Charles wouldn't turn out to be a creeper.

Charles stepped forward, hand extended. "Pleasure to meet you, Miss Loretta. Pete told me all about you."

"He did, huh?" Loretta replied, cutting her eyes at Pete.

"All good, Miss Loretta," Pete assured her. "All good."

Before anyone could say anything else, a soft voice greeted them from the porch. "Heeeey."

Everyone looked up to find Vashawn standing on the porch, her left hip jutted out to give her baby a seat as he grasped her T-shirt. "Miss Loretta, you brought the party, huh?"

"I'm sorry, baby," Loretta said. "This was the only time Pete could come. He was spendin' time with his family and had to bring them with him."

"It's good," Vashawn said. "Long as that noise stops and we can sleep tonight, y'all can bring whoever y'all want."

"You sure, young lady?" Donovan asked. "Me and my brother can wait outside if you're not comfortable."

"No, it's cold out here. Y'all good. Come on in."

"Okay, thank you," Pete said as he led the procession into the house. "We shouldn't be too long. My uncle knows a lil somethin' about repairs, too."

"Yeah, I taught Pete everything he knows," Charles said, following his nephew to the back of the house.

Loretta caught herself rolling her eyes upward as she followed the men to the vent. She could already see that Uncle Charles was going to work her last nerve. The last thing she needed was some tagalong trying to inject his opinion. Hopefully this would go quickly.

When they reached the vent, she caught Charles giving the crown molding an approving nod.

"You own this?" he asked.

"Yes," Loretta, said, slightly defensive.

"Nice."

"Thank you."

He let out a low whistle. "A woman about her business. I like that."

She winced, arms folded. "Aren't you supposed to be helpin' your nephew?"

"Don't mind my brother, Sister Willis," Donovan said quickly. "All these years of being single and he still don't know how to keep his mouth closed."

"Mm-hmm. I see."

Pete removed the vent cover while Charles leaned casually in the doorway, watching Loretta.

"So, you do this full-time?" he asked.

"Do what? Own property?" she asked. "I own three properties."

"I didn't know that, Miss Loretta," Vashawn interjected. She sat on the bed, feeding the baby through a small bottle. Loretta didn't miss those days at all. "You got it goin' on."

Loretta smiled until she heard Charles say, "She certainly does."

Her smile quickly became a grimace.

Pete looked up from the vent. "Looks like it's just loose framing. I can tighten this up now. I have a few extra screws in my toolbox. Shouldn't take more than a few minutes."

Charles leaned in and looked over Pete's shoulder. He pointed at a rusty screw hanging onto the vent for dear life. "Now, *this* right here is your problem. This screw is barely hanging on. I betcha that's what's causing the vibration. Common issue."

Loretta furrowed her brows. "Isn't that what Pete just said, but in fewer words?"

"I just wanted to make sure you understood what's goin' on," Charles pushed. "These rusty screws will cause you problems every time."

"Charles, come on over here and stand with me," Donovan suggested, beckoning him to the doorway.

"Good idea," Loretta mumbled.

"One day you're gonna have to teach me how I can get my own houses," Vashawn said, bouncing her baby boy on her lap despite the loud hum of Pete's power drill. "This waitressin' stuff is for the birds."

"It's not easy," Loretta said. "You gotta ma—"

"The key to ownin' these old houses is to make sure you check the filters monthly," Charles interrupted. "If you don't, your whole system could shut down. Gotta keep it clean, air flowing."

Before Loretta could respond, Pete stood, wiped his hands, and picked up his tools. "All done. I'ma go on and get all these people out your house, Vashawn. I see you're tryin' to get your baby to sleep."

"Yeah, he's tired," she replied. "He didn't get a lot of sleep last night because of the noise."

"Well, you shouldn't have to worry about that anymore," Pete assured her.

"If you do, you know you can call me," Loretta added.

The group proceeded back to the front door, with Vashawn bringing up the rear, still bouncing her baby.

"Thank y'all again for comin' so quick," she said. "If I don't see y'all again, have a Happy New Year."

"And Happy New Year to you, my baby," Loretta replied hugging her tenant. She then looked down at the baby and gave him an exaggerated smile. "You make sure you take care of Mommy."

"So precious," Loretta mumbled as she followed the men out of the house. She trudged down the steps to the driveway. A stream of heat ran up her back, and she turned around to see Charles leaning against Pete's truck, staring at her. It gave her the creeps. "Um, nice meeting you, Mr. Charles."

"Oh, the pleasure was *all* mine," he replied with a smile.

Uncle Charles!" Pete called from his truck's driver's seat. "We gotta go, man."

"One sec, nephew," Charles said, walking toward Loretta.

Loretta stood her ground and crossed her arms as he drew closer. "May I help you, Mr. Charles?"

He smiled, but to Loretta it didn't look friendly. It looked slick, like there were plans rolling around in his mind. What was wrong with the men her age? Did they ever grow out of their player instincts? Charles was the third man she'd met in a matter of days who thought he was *Return of the Mack*. As much as she liked that song years ago, she hated it right now.

"Why are you so defensive?" he asked. "I'm just talkin'. That okay?"

"I've got things to do, Mr. Charles," she stated, avoiding eye contact. To keep her hands busy, she opened her car door and threw her purse on the seat. "I'm not here for entertainment."

"You could probably use some entertainment. Uptight for no reason."

"I don't want to go out with you, Mr. Charles."

"Fair enough," Charles said. "But for the record, I wasn't gonna ask you out."

Loretta diverted her eyes again, slightly embarrassed for assuming. That app had her mind all messed up. "Weren't you just talkin' about entertainment?"

"I did, and you're beautiful, but I didn't mean *I* was gonna take you out. I just made an observation.

She rolled her eyes and raised an eyebrow. "You slick, I'll give you that."

"Charles, bruh, let's go!" Donovan called. Charles looked back at his brother and nephew and then back at Loretta, the same slick smile pasted on his face.

"You're a good woman, Miss Loretta," he said, backing toward the truck. "You don't meet a lot of women who got their life in order and don't apologize for it. That's rare."

"At my age, why *wouldn't* I have my life together? Loretta asked as she stepped into her car.

"You'd be surprised," he replied, closing her car door behind her. She started the motor and powered down her window.

"Well," she said, again averting his eyes, "make yourself useful and tell your nephew I'm gonna need him tomorrow to help me set up for the party."

He leaned into the car and rested his elbows in the window seal. "I'll do that. And I'll stay out your way. Unless you invite me."

She grimaced. "Don't hold your breath."

He maintained his smile and tapped the window seal as he stood up. Loretta watched him from her rearview mirror as he climbed into the backseat of the truck. She couldn't hear them talking, but Donovan seemed to be fussing at him. He didn't look angry, but he didn't look pleased, either. *Get him, Brother Randall!*

Chapter 9

"Girl, wake up!" Liza shouted, snatching Maya from her tenth hour of sleep.

Maya sat up and groaned. Why couldn't her mother just let her sleep? She was on winter break, and she ended the semester with straight As. Didn't she deserve the right to be lazy for a couple weeks?

"Are you up?" Liza's voice sailed through the bedroom door.

"Yes, Mom!" Maya yelled back.

Maya sat on the edge of her bed and straightened her hair bonnet, which had repositioned itself countless times as she slept. Her notebook lay on the floor next to her feet. She kicked it to the side, her sight too blurry to read anything.

She stood and stretched from side to side, and then reached for her phone. Maybe the white noise of Sirius Radio would get her moving. Although she had no idea what she needed to get moving for. Christmas was over, and the New Year's Eve party wasn't for another few days. Maybe she'd call Myron and see what he had going today. That thought left as quickly as it came once her paternal grandmother's voice entered her head: *Don't you be runnin' to no doors for no man. He can wait.*

Between Grandma Sylvia trying to get her to be a Southern belle, Grams trying to get her to be independent, and her parents trying to get her to get a job, she needed a break. She would graduate from college in less than two years, and all she wanted to do was have some fun before starting her career and officially becoming an adult.

How could she do that with her parents in her ear? Most parents wanted their kids to just concentrate on their studies while they were in college, but not hers. *You need to be more responsible. Start thinking about your future.* Why couldn't they realize she was *already* thinking about her future?

Running out and getting a job at Smoothie King or something would just disrupt her master plan. She wanted to have fun while making her own money. The little money she made from doing her friends' hair in the dorms was good for fast food runs and groceries, but she wanted more.

Her goal was to pay off her student loans within two years of graduation. She wanted to travel before starting medical school. She also wanted to move and work for a hospital in DC, the center of Black excellence. Doing a couple heads a week wasn't going to get her there.

She opened her door and carried her phone to the bathroom. She stared into the mirror and snatched off her bonnet. Her cornrows were still intact. Once she got dressed, she'd take down the braids and shape her hair into a beautiful curly crown.

"How did that one girl take her hair down? She didn't have *no* frizz," she mumbled, as she scrolled though YouTube. Her fingers flew across the screen as she searched for the video thumbnail. Just as she found it, her phone rang. She smiled when she saw Myron's name appear on the screen. *Guess I don't have to wait for him to call me,* she thought as she hit the TALK button.

"Hey, you," she greeted, walking back to her bedroom. She flopped onto her bed and threw her feet in the air.

"Hey, pretty lady," Myron said, his voice as deep and smooth as chocolate ice cream. "Watcha up to?"

"Not much. About to do my hair."

"You be killin' the natural hair game," Myron said. "Always lookin' good."

Maya's blush warmed her face. "You think so?"

"Fa sho. You could be makin' way more money."

"I don't have time to do any more heads than what I'm doing," Maya said. "I barely have time to study as it is."

"But that's the thing," Myron pushed. "You don't have to do any more heads."

Maya scrunched her eyebrows. "Huh?"

"Sweety, don't you know how many people are making money on YouTube and Instagram now? All you have to do is record yourself doing your own hair or record yourself doing your girls' hair and post the videos. If enough people see it, maybe you can get monetized."

"I don't know, bae," Maya said, biting the inside of her cheek. "That sounds like a lot of work. The YouTubers I watch have like thousands of followers and post new videos like three times a week."

"Yeah, that does sound like a lot," Myron agreed. "Well, just think about it. I know you've been lookin' for more ways to make some money."

"Yeah, that's true," Maya said, popping up from her bed. She began searching her closet for an out for the day. "So, is that why you called? To give me business advice?"

He laughed. "Nah, I just wanted to see if you wanted to go to a movie later.

"Oh, you wanna see *Wicked*?" Maya exclaimed.

No, thank you. I'll leave that to you and your girls. I was thinkin' *Lord of the Rings*."

"Oh," Maya replied, the enthusiasm gone from her voice. "Sure."

Myron laughed and sighed. "You really wanna see the Wizard of Oz?"

"It's not the *Wizard of Oz*. It's the wicked witch's story. You get to hear what happened from her point of view."

"That's interesting."

"So, can we see it? Please?"

"Only if we can watch *Lord of the Rings* tomorrow," Myron relented. "You owe me."

Maya squealed in excitement. "I got you, bae!"

Just as Maya was about to confirm the time of the movie, Liza called her from the kitchen. "Maya, your grandma's coming over in a bit!"

"Okay!" she called back. She turned back to her conversation. "I gotta go, bae. Grams is on the way over. Text me and let me know what time you're comin' to get me."

"Okay. It'll be later this evening. I'm about to go to a Kwanzaa get-together with some of my frat brothers."

"Oh, that's cool. Today's the third day, isn't it?"

"Very good," Myron said. "It's Ujima, which means collective work and responsibility. It's about community building and solving problems together."

Maya laughed. "Is that why you're over there tryin' to help me make money?"

Myron laughed with her. "I guess you can say that."

"You got inspired and now you wanna inspire me?"

"Anything wrong with that?"

"Nothin' at all," Maya said with a smile.

* * *

By the time Loretta arrived that afternoon, Maya had finished her hair and was sitting in the kitchen making a salad.

"I meant to tell y'all," she said as she sliced a buttery soft avocado. "Myron suggested I start a YouTube channel for natural hair."

"That's interesting," Liza replied as she sipped her coffee.

"There's people doing hair on YouTube?" Loretta asked.

"The community is huge," Maya said. "I follow like ten naturalistas, but there are a bunch more."

"Natur-what?"

"Naturalistas, Momma," Liza said. "It's what they call women who are good at doing natural hair."

"Right," Maya confirmed. "I told him I didn't have time for it, but I'm kinda thinkin' about it."

"Girl, you don't have time for that foolishness," Liza dismissed.

Maya made a face at her. "It's not foolishness, Momma. There are women making serious money on social media."

"I know, but you've gotta be consistent with it. You don't even wake up at the same time every day."

"Ooo, she got you there, My My," Loretta said, propping her chin in her hand.

"Grams!" Maya exclaimed.

Loretta laughed. "I'm just kidding, baby. You really think you could do this?"

"I'm thinkin' about trying."

Liza nodded. "You serious about this?"

Maya shrugged.

"Well, why don't you start on your Instagram page? Post a couple of videos and see what happens. YouTube is a big move, and it might be better for you to build an audience first."

Maya nodded, taking in her mother's words. "I can do that."

She looked at Loretta and smiled. "Can I start with you, Grams?"

"Me?" Loretta asked, her eyes wide with surprise. She patted her low afro puff. "Child, I got a hair appointment Monday."

"Well, that just means if you don't like it, you already have an appointment to get it fixed," Liza suggested.

"She's gonna like it," Maya said confidently. "Grams always likes when I do her hair."

Loretta sighed. "Well, since you got me all out on the Internet, you might as well put me on your lil Instagram channel."

"Yes!" Maya exclaimed, jumping up from the table. "This is some real Ujima stuff right here!"

"Goodness, looks like the Kwanzaa spirit has gotten to her, too," Loretta said with a laugh.

"I see," Liza agreed.

Maya ran upstairs to the bathroom and grabbed curling cream, mousse, and her spray bottle. She tucked the bottles into the bend of her left arm, and then grabbed a rat tail comb, a wide-tooth comb and a paddle brush from the vanity drawer and slipped them into her pocket.

She skipped back down the steps and placed everything on the coffee table. She then ran back to her room, pulled out her ring light, and took it back to the living room, where she positioned it in the middle of the room. She then went to the kitchen and dragged a chair into the living room next to the ring light.

"I'm ready, Grams!" she called out.

Loretta stepped into the living room and froze, hands on her hips. "Now, what is all this?"

"Let's just say it's my studio," Maya said proudly, tapping the chair. "Come. Sit."

Loretta squinted at her granddaughter. "You better not make me look like one of them Instagram girls."

"I won't," Maya said. "You're gonna look better than you did when you went on your date with your saxophone friend."

"Don't even bring him up," Loretta said, waving her hand. Liza giggled.

Loretta narrowed her eyes. "And no wild baby hairs, either."

"Lord, please no," Liza added, holding up her hand.

"No ma'am," Maya said, holding back a laugh.

For the next hour, they talked and laughed as Maya parted and twisted Loretta's long, gray, fluffy hair. Maya's fingers moved swiftly through her grandmother's tresses, spraying each section with rose and aloe water before applying mousse and curling cream and braiding it into slightly tight cornrow. Liza assisted by moving the ring light around and using Maya's phone to zoom in on her hands as she worked.

Once she the last cornrow was in place, Maya set up her hairdryer   on   the   dining   room   table.

"Okay, Grams, you gotta sit under here for about forty minutes," Maya explained as she pulled the hood of the dryer over Loretta's head.

"Very professional, Loretta commented. "All I need is a glass of wine."

"I got you!" Liza said, walking to the kitchen. A few minutes later she reemerged with a glass of white wine. "I know you like Malbec, but all we have is Chardonnay right now."

"As long as it's not sweet wine, I'm good," Loretta said, accepting the wine. "But you know red is good for your heart."

"I'll keep that in mind," Liza said, sitting on the armchair next to her mother.

Maya sat on the coffee table across from Loretta and pointed her phone at her. "Grams, what kind of hairstyles did you wear back in the day?"

Loretta smiled and looked upward as she recalled her younger days. She took a sip of her wine and began, "Wooo, child, that was so long ago. I was born in the fifties, so it was pigtails until I got to high school. Your great grandmother used to hot comb our hair every Saturday so our hair shined for church Sunday morning. That comb would be so hot that flames would still be on it when she pulled it from the fire. She would whip it through the air to cool it off, but it would still sizzle when it touched the grease in our hair."

"Grandmother used to comb my hair with that same comb in the eighties," Liza interjected. Maya swung the phone to her mother as she spoke. "I hated that thing, and I still have the burn marks on my ears to show it."

Loretta chuckled, and the camera went back to her. "I didn't like it too hot either. When I got old enough, I began wearing my hair in afros. Our afros weren't like what you young girls are wearing now. They were round and fluffy. We didn't have twist-outs and braid-outs and coil-outs. We used to call it a bush."

"Like the Black Panthers and afro picks with the fist?"

Loretta laughed again. "Something like that. Now, I gotta admit that when the Jheri curls came around in the eighties, I was all in. My curls were gorgeous! Your momma had them, too."

"Momma, you had a soul glow?" Maya exclaimed, thinking back to the curly haired family on Eddie Murphy's *Coming to America.*

"Yep, and I looked good!" Liza said, smiling.

"I don't even remember when we stopped getting those Jheri curls," Loretta said. "What I do know is that we didn't have to cut our hair off to get them because our hair was already natural. The girls with the relaxers, on the other hand, had to cut all of their relaxed hair—we used to call them perms—off because you can't process a curl on top of relaxed hair. So, while everybody else was walkin' around bald-headed, your momma and I had length!"

Maya and Liza laughed and clapped.

"One thing I did learn through my hair evolution, though, is you don't need chemicals to be beautiful," Loretta said. "Your hair is a gift from God."

Maya smiled and turned off her camera. "Love that. All of this is goin' on my IG page. You are givin' me content for days, and we haven't even finished your hair yet!"

"What are you plannin' on puttin' on your page?" Liza asked.

"For now, probably just tutorials, tips, and demos."

Loretta nodded. "I'm really proud of you. I hope it works out for you."

Maya reached over and squeezed Loretta's knee. "Thanks, Grams."

The hair dryer cut off a few minutes later. Maya lifted the hood and used two fingers to squeeze each cornrow to check for dryness. Once she was sure they were all dry, she squeezed some olive oil into her hands, rubbed them together, and carefully unraveled each braid. Once she finished, Loretta's hair was styled in a soft, fluffy twist-out with tapered sides. A small braid hung from each temple with a little pop of gold hair cuffs.

Maya gave Loretta a handheld mirror to check out her new hairstyle. Loretta took the mirror and stared for a moment, blinking.

"You love it?" Liza asked.

"You brought me back to the seventies, child. I was a bad girl back then."

Maya beamed. "That was the idea."

Loretta turned and touched Maya's cheek. "Baby, you've got somethin' here. You've got real talent."

"Thanks, Grams," Maya said, hugging Loretta. "Maybe when Mom takes out her braids, she'll let me do her hair, too."

"I'll consider it," Liza said, folding her arms.

Maya took a few photos of the finished style while Loretta posed. Just before leaving for her date with Myron, she posted her grandmother's hair photo with a caption:

On this third Day of Kwanzaa, I celebrate my grandmother, who let me style her hair in this bangin' braid-out. Grams is the blueprint—and now she's the model. Face card never declines. #Ujima #NaturalHairLegacy #GrandmaGlow #SundayBest

Chapter 10

Loretta's twist-out was the talk of the congregation at Second Greater Mount Calvary Baptist Church Sunday. As soon as she walked into the church, the compliments sailed through the air.

"Look at you, Sister Willis! Lookin' good!"

"New look, huh?"

"I love it. My hair never stays fluffy like that."

Loretta accepted the compliments with grace, but she started feeling slightly self-conscious. Was she attracting *too much* attention? Were the other sisters in the church going to think she was being ridiculous?

"You look good, Grandma," Maya whispered as she, Loretta, Liza, and David settled into their usual spot on the third pew, left-hand side. Maya sat between her mother and grandmother, unable to take her eyes off her handywork.

"Well, I like lookin' good, but I feel like everyone's staring at me," Loretta whispered back.

"They know a queen when they see one," Maya replied with a proud smile.

Loretta smiled back just as the choir stood. "You did good, baby."

Liza smiled as she peeped around Maya and whispered, "You *do* look beautiful, Momma."

Loretta closed her eyes and swayed back and forth as the choir sang their rendition of Richard Smallwood's *The Center of My Joy*. She'd always loved this song. It reminded her of her first couple of years trying to cope with the silence after James died. She'd never realized how loud silence could be. It was deafening at first, and not even her workouts could quell the noise. Had it not been for prayer and Bible study, she wasn't sure she could have made it. She'd always seen her relationship with God as the center of her life, but that time grew her closer to Him in a way she hadn't realized before.

Loretta opened her eyes and looked around as the choir drew to a close. Some people swayed in their seats, some sat still, and others, including Liza and David, stood with their hands in the air in praise. The Spirit was definitely in the place.

A movement and whispers from behind captured her attention. She looked back and was shocked to see Pete and Charles scooting through the pew behind her. They took a seat directly behind her and Charles had the nerve to smile! *What was he doing here? And why were they so late?*

She nodded a quick greeting, reasoning that it only made sense for him to be at church. Pete and his parents were members. Why *wouldn't* they invite Charles to church?

He had on a dark gray suit, a crisp black shirt, and a gray tie. He looked good, with his old Danny Glover-looking self. But she'd never give him the satisfaction of telling him that. His ego was big enough and didn't need any help from her.

* * *

After service, Loretta and her family mingled outside on the church steps with the other members, chatting about Christmas and their plans for New Year's Eve. The cool weather whipped through their coats, but it didn't deter the kids from running circles around the parking lot.

"Girl, you shoulda seen that string of a bracelet he called himself givin' me," one of the younger members told Maya. "Talk about ugly! Like I wasn't gonna find out he gave a real necklace to Keisha."

Maya shook her head and pursed her lips. "These dudes."

"Right?" the girl agreed.

"Y'all are rough on these young boys," David commented.

Maya looked up, unaware that he'd been listening. "How you gonna talk, Daddy? You're the one who said we shouldn't let up."

"You're right, I said that," David said, facing his daughter and her friend. "But you gotta know when to apply pressure and when to walk away. Ain't no need to be fightin' for something that ain't worth it. If you know your lil friend is messin' with somebody else, why you foolin' with him?"

Loretta laughed as the two girls pursed their lips and looked away. She didn't miss her twenties at all.

She looked around just in time to see Charles and Pete walking toward her. Charles looked even better standing up. She looked away to keep from staring.

"Miss Loretta," he said, approaching.

She turned. "Mr. Charles."

He nodded once. "Happy Sunday mornin' to you."

"Same to you."

"What's up, young man?" David greeted Pete. They gave each other a bruh man handshake. "You lookin' good."

"Thanks, Mr. David," Pete replied. "Tryna be like you."

As the two men talked with each other, Loretta and Charles just stared at each other. Maya and her friend cut their eyes at each other, not knowing whether to worry or laugh.

"Miss Loretta, mind takin' a walk with me?" Charles asked finally.

Loretta looked at her family, who looked concerned. Pete, on the other hand, looked interested. "Y'all can go on ahead. I'll meet y'all in a few."

"Ummm, who is that?" Liza asked, folding her arms.

"Oh, that's my Uncle Charles," Pete explained quickly. "He's visitin' us for the holidays."

"Habari gani, Uncle Charles," Liza said, staring him down. "How you know my momma?"

"Excuse me?" Loretta cut in, placing her hands on her hips. "Ain't you 'bout nothin'. I met Mr. Charles through Pete yesterday. Now, leave me be and let me have my conversation."

"Sorry, Momma Loretta," David said with a laugh. "We'll see you later."

"Wait, I've got questions," Liza protested.

"And they'll be answered later," her husband interjected as he pulled her away. "Now, let's go. The game is on."

Pete backed away. "I'ma go find my parents and my wife. They been in that church for a minute."

"Guess I'll see you later," Maya told her friend as she followed her parents.

"I'll call you later, girl," her friend said.

Charles chuckled as Loretta's family walked away. "You got a beautiful family."

"Yes, I do," Loretta agreed. "So, how can I help you?"

Charles placed his hand slightly on Loretta's waist and ushered her onto the sidewalk. The touch surprised her, but she quickly relaxed.

"My brother and nephew say I owe you an apology," Charles said as they strolled.

Loretta raised an eyebrow. "For what?"

"I came on too strong at the rental. Didn't mean to offend."

Loretta stopped walking and crossed her arms slowly. "But you did."

He nodded. "Looks like they were right."

"But," she continued, "I appreciate the apology."

"I was just tryin' to be helpful," he said. A bashful smile crossed his face. "And a lil funny."

She laughed. "And you were neither."

Charles smiled. "You a cold woman, Miss Loretta."

Loretta almost smiled back. "I'm actually quite friendly."

"Maybe I can experience that friendly side one of these days."

Loretta raised her eyebrows and changed the subject. "You enjoy the service today?"

"It was good. Your pastor spoke well."

"Yes, Pastor Lewis brought it today."

"Yes, he did. Y'all have a beautiful church."

He cut his eyes at Loretta and smirked. "With some beautiful members."

Loretta gasped, her mouth open as she tried to hold back a laugh. She certainly wasn't expecting to enjoy this conversation, but here she was.

"Sorry," he said with a chuckle. "I couldn't help myself."

Loretta chuckled in spite of herself.

"Can you allow me to take you to lunch?" Charles asked. "No pressure."

She hesitated.

"Please? I promise I'm not a bad guy."

She softened a bit. "I don't think you are."

"Good, then you'll let me take you to lunch?"

Loretta smiled and glanced up. *James, you did this, didn't you?* "Sure. Let's go. But in the spirit of Ujamaa, let's support a Black-owned restaurant."

Charles brought both hands to his heart in mock joy. "The great Loretta Willis is about to let me take her to lunch! Let's go before you change your mind."

She giggled, drawing more flirtation.

"And she smiled? This is a real belated Christmas miracle."

"Maybe it's a Kwanzaa miracle," Loretta corrected.

Charles nodded, impressed. "We'll have to talk about that over lunch. Did you drive to church, or should I drive you? Donovan let me steal his car for the day."

"I drove," she replied, walking back to the church parking lot. "Tell me where we're goin' and I'll meet you there."

"Just follow me, woman," he replied, speeding his pace. He cut his eyes at her as he passed her and mumbled, "Doggone independent women."

"I heard that!" she called after him.

* * *

Loretta followed Charles into the parking lot of The Big Easy Kitchen, a small restaurant near City Park. It seemed to be a quaint place with an unassuming façade. She pulled into a parking space near the back of the restaurant and got out of the car. Charles joined her a few seconds later.

"Nice place," she said, staring at the doorway of the restaurant.

"You been here before?" he asked.

"No, I don't think I've even heard of this place."

"Nice, then I get to show you somethin' new. I saw this place featured on the *Food Network*. I wanted to try it so I thought today would be as a good a day as any."

Loretta nodded. "*Food Network*, huh? I'm game."

They walked into the restaurant together. Loretta was immediately struck by the ornate décor that looked more upscale than casual. Mellow jazz music played from unseen speakers, and scents of roasted garlic, smoked paprika, and something spicy filled the air.

The restaurant was filled with patrons who didn't appear to be from New Orleans. New Orleanians had a look, and these people didn't have it. But then again, if this place had been featured on the *Food Network*, there was a sure bet these people were tourists.

"Hi, welcome to the Big Easy Kitchen," the hostess greeted. "Do y'all have a reservation?"

"No, did we need one?" Charles replied.

"No, you're okay," she said with a smile. "We have space today."

"Lucky us," Loretta remarked as they followed the hostess to a table near a window with a striking view of the live oak trees that populated City Park.

"What's on your mind?"

Loretta was startled, realizing she'd been staring out the window longer than she realized. "Just lookin' at the trees. City Park is one of my favorite places."

To her, the park was one of the most beautiful places in New Orleans, with its ponds, sculpture garden, and walking trails.

There was even a carousel in the park. Loretta took Liza there often when she was a little girl.

The waitress came and took their drink orders. Loretta ordered her usual Malbec, and Charles ordered a beer.

"Glad you're pleased," he said with a smile. "I'm surprised you've never been here before."

"I haven't been to *every* restaurant in the city," Loretta said with a laugh. "I enjoy cooking. I leave the restaurants to the tourists unless it's a special occasion."

"Oh, so you cook?" he asked, picking up a menu. "What's your favorite thing to cook?"

"Gumbo, of course. And I make a good pound cake."

"Nice, I love a good gumbo," he replied with a smile. He began reading the menu. "Looks like this place has three kinds of gumbo. One is vegan. Interesting. I ain't eatin' that one."

Vegan? Loretta's face twitched. She turned the menu over and read the about section. This was Henri's restaurant! This city was too darn small.

Charles didn't seem to notice her conundrum. "I heard the chef is the owner. He used to work at a couple fancy spots around town and decided to open his own place."

"Yeah, he gets around," she mumbled. She skimmed the menu and felt the tension in her shoulders rise. She'd been dating for less than a week and had already found herself in a pickle. Of all the places in New Orleans Charles could have taken her, he chose Henri's place. And Henri had been on *Food Network*? What were the chances?

Well, one thing was for sure. If his menu was any indication, his accolades were well deserved. She decided to relax and enjoy a good meal. Maybe he would be too busy to see her. Or maybe he wasn't even there.

"You strike me as a seafood lady," Charles said, placing his menu back on the table. "Am I right?"

"I like a good shrimp or two," she replied, "but I think I'm going to try that vegan gumbo. I've heard you can't tell the difference."

"Huh?" I thought you hadn't been here before?"

"I realized I've met the chef before. He raved about that gumbo."

"Really now," he said, nodding and leaning back. Loretta knew he was slightly confused, but she wasn't about to explain. She didn't owe him anything.

The waitress returned with their drinks and asked for their meal orders.

"I'll have the sea bass and okra, and the lady will have the vegan gumbo," Charles said.

"Excellent choices," the waitress said. "Those dishes have won awards."

"Nice," he replied. "Should be good."

"For sure," the waitress said as she turned away.

Loretta smiled, actually excited about tasting Henri's famous vegan gumbo. *It better be good.* She turned and caught a glimpse of the open kitchen, and there he was. Henri. His hands moving swiftly and expertly as he prepared a dish while supervising his staff. She could see his lips moving but couldn't make out what he was saying. He certainly didn't look like the same inappropriate man who had taken her out for lunch the day after Christmas.

He looked up, his eyes sweeping the dining room, and then looked down. He looked up again and their eyes locked. He didn't smile or frown. Instead, he watched her for a second, raised his eyebrows, and then turned back to the plate he was preparing as if nothing happened. Loretta blinked and cleared her throat.

"You okay?" Charles asked.

"Um, yes," she replied absently. "Just saw someone I know."

"My competition?" he joked.

Loretta looked at him and gave him a half smile. "Hardly."

"Well, if it's no one I need to worry about, I'm gonna enjoy my lunch date with the beautiful lady sittin' in front of me."

Loretta cocked her head to the side. "You've got a lot of confidence, don't you?"

"Always have."

"How come you never got married again?"

"You just jump right in there, don't you?"

"Sorry," she relented. "Probably too personal too soon."

He took a sip from his beer. "No, it's okay. I just felt like it was easier to stay single. I know you've never experienced it before, but divorce takes a lot outta you. So instead of goin' through all that again, I decided to just concentrate on me."

"You got a girlfriend?" Loretta asked with a smirk. She was sure she knew the answer to that question.

"Nope."

"Really, now?"

"Really."

Loretta leaned back and sipped her wine. She wasn't sure she believed him, but she had no reason not to. Her eyes involuntarily traveled back to the kitchen, but Henri was gone. She breathed a sigh of relief, feeling the microscope she'd been under finally been lifted.

A sommelier appeared a moment later with a bottle of red wine. "Chef's compliments."

Loretta blinked again. *Smooth, Henri. Real smooth.*

Charles raised an eyebrow. "I guess your friend the chef knows you're here."

Loretta chuckled politely, but her nervous eyes lingered on the kitchen as if waiting for Henri to reappear. "I guess so."

Chapter 11

Monday morning, the day before the New Year's Eve party and the fifth day of Kwanzaa—also known as Nia—would prove to be a busy one. Loretta had to finalize plans with the caterer and finish decorating the house for the party.

Although Maya had saved her a little time by doing her hair on Saturday, she needed a refresh. Her granddaughter would be coming over later to take care of her hair, but what her makeshift stylist didn't know was that she'd also be putting her to work around the house.

Loretta started the day with a three-mile power walk to get the blood flowing, followed by a hot cup of coffee. As she sat at the kitchen bar sipping from her liquid energy, she opened Amazon.com on her phone and scrolled through last-minute decorations she could get delivered by the next day. A new outfit or two wouldn't hurt either. Two hundred forty-six dollars and sixty-seven cents later, she tapped checkout and closed the app.

Out of habit, she opened the dating app and checked her messages. Nothing from Marcus or Henri. A couple of creepy messages, which she deleted immediately. And one new one from a man named Everett. She opened it to find a photo of a clean-cut, distinguished gentleman with caramel skin. He wore a suit and held a short glass of something brown. Probably some type of cognac. *Hmmm, very nice.*

His message was respectful and unassuming. *I know it's still early, but in case you don't answer my message, I want to wish you a Happy New Year. You have a beautiful smile. I wish you many more smiles in the coming year.*

"Nice, Everett," Loretta mumbled, nodding. She took another sip from her coffee. Her eyes went back to Henri, surprised she hadn't heard from him. That bottle of wine was a nice move. It would be rude to not acknowledge it.

She tapped on his name and typed, *Thank you for the wine yesterday. Very nice of you. And I have to admit the vegan gumbo was delicious, but I won't be replacing my recipe anytime soon.*

She set down her phone and gulped the last of her coffee. Maya should be popping up any minute now. Maybe she'd make them a little breakfast. She stood up and opened the refrigerator. Eggs and sausage. Good. She opened the cabinet and found half a box of grits and a full box of pancake mix. They had options. She'd let Maya decide what they'd eat when she arrived.

In the meantime, she stood in the middle of the kitchen and took a mental check of her to do list. Before she could get to the second item, she heard the latch turn on the front door.

"Grams!" Maya shouted. "You here?"

"Girl, of course I'm here," Loretta replied. "I'm in the kitchen."

"Perfect," Maya said, entering the kitchen. She set a large shoulder bag on the counter.

"Your momma drop you off?"

"Yes, Ma'am. She had to go into the office today, so she dropped me here on the way."

Loretta nodded and eyed Maya's bag. "What's all that?"

"Hair products. And my ring light."

"You're taking this social media thing pretty seriously, aren't you?"

"Grams, you won't believe this, but that photo I posted of you the other day got like a thousand likes and four thousand views," Maya announced, holding up her phone.

"What?" Loretta gasped. "Are you serious?"

She grabbed the phone from her granddaughter and stared at the screen. Sure enough, the number one thousand seven hundred and two sat next to a little heart, and six hundred fifty-three sat next to the comment bubble. Nervously she tapped the comments to see what people had to say.

Body_365: *Yes, Grams!*

Shannonthecreator: *Now this is how an afro is s'posed to look!*

DaliaT: *I wanna be her when I'm a grandma.*

"Well, this is," Loretta mumbled, scrolling through the comments, "interesting."

"Grams, can you believe I got like two hundred new followers from just this one post?" Maya announced, bouncing in excitement. "We've gotta do a follow-up."

"Well, since you're refreshing my hair today, you can get some more content, but baby, I'm not gonna be your model every time you gotta post something."

"I know, and you don't have to be. I'm going to have diverse content. Some of myself, some of my customers at school, and maybe every once in a while you could make an appearance?"

Loretta sighed. "I guess as long as it's every once in a while."

"Thanks, Grams!" Maya sang, wrapping her arms around her grandmother's neck and kissing her on the cheek. "I love you."

"Girl, get away from me with all that," Loretta remarked, playfully pulling Maya's arms from around her. "Between you and your momma, y'all got me all over the Internet."

"You're a star!"

Loretta responded by pursing her lips and wrinkling her nose. "I wouldn't say all that."

"What's under your scarf right now?" Maya asked, reaching for the silk scarf covering Loretta's hair.

"Excuse you!" Loretta snapped, snatching her head away from her daughter's grasp.

"Come on, Grams," Maya pleaded. "It's just you and me here. I just wanna see what I'll be workin' with later."

"I guess," Loretta relented. "I just have it in two big cornrows to keep it from tangling."

"That's good. Those tangles can be the devil and can dry out your hair and break it off."

"You do know I was doing my hair long before you decided to be a beauty expert, right?"

Maya laughed and removed Loretta's scarf from her head. "You gonna do anything with it right now?"

"I probably should. Pete will be over soon to help with the decorations."

"Ooo! Can I put it in a quick style just for now? I can do something else with it later tonight."

Loretta looked skeptical. "Like what?"

"It'll be simple and cute," Maybe said, setting her ring light on the table. "I'm gonna make you a headband."

"Huh?"

"Watch. You'll see."

Loretta sighed as she sat. Maya turned on the ring light and propped her phone on the stand. After hitting record, Maya squeezed olive oil into her hands and began using her fingers to unravel Loretta's braids. Once Loretta's gray tresses flowed, Maya picked up a rattail comb and parted her hair from ear to ear, and then cornrowed the part down, making it look like a headband. She left the rest of her hair in a fluffy afro.

"What do you think?" Maya asked, holding a mirror in front of her.

Loretta took the mirror and moved her head back and forth to inspect the hairstyle. It was nothing she would have chosen for herself, but it wasn't bad. "It's cute. I swear you're tryin' to turn me into a spring chicken."

"Stop playin', Grams," Maya quipped, taking the mirror from her. "You don't even look seventy. Probably why you've had so much luck on that dating app. And why Pete's uncle was makin' sweet eyes at you at church yesterday."

"Sweet eyes?"

"Ummm, yeah. That man couldn't wait to steal you away from us."

Loretta giggled in spite of herself. Ole Uncle Charles did show a different side of himself yesterday. And he did say he wanted to see her again before he went back to Houston. But sweet eyes from a forever bachelor? She wasn't sure about that. "I didn't think you saw all that."

"Everybody did," Maya said as she placed her hair products back into the bag. "We all thought it was cute."

Loretta shook her head and changed the subject. "Well, we got a lot of work to do to get this house in order for tomorrow. I'ma have to put you to work for now."

"I figured," Maya replied. "That's why I wanted to come early. Is it okay if Myron swings by a little later to help?"

"Why not? The more, the merrier."

Maya followed her grandmother to the guest room, which held the rest of the decorations for the party.

"Wow, Grams," Maya said, eying the packages of colorful hats and streamers. She picked up a pink synthetic wig and tried it on. "You're goin' all out this year, huh?"

Loretta chuckled a little. "I figured as crazy as this year is turnin' out, why not do a lil somethin' different."

"I hear you," Maya said, tossing the package back on the bed just as the doorbell rang.

"That must be Pete," Loretta guessed, turning toward the bedroom door. "Go ahead and gather this stuff up and put it on the dining room table and start makin' giftbags."

Loretta left the room before Maya could protest and walked straight to the front door. Her business demeanor suddenly morphed into an unexpected smile when she opened the door and saw Charles standing there.

"Good mornin', Miss Loretta," he greeted, leaning on her door frame. He smiled as his eyes travelled from her fluffy hair to her wrinkled T-shirt, to her black sweatpants, to her fuzzy slippers. "You're lookin' pretty radiant."

She blushed and waved her hand at him, thanking God she'd let Maya do her hair. "Stop that. I'm a mess."

Charles chuckled as Pete walked up next to him. "Learn to take a compliment, woman. I've officially seen you dressed up and dressed down, and you're still lookin' good."

"'Scuse me," Pete said, sticking his head between them. "Y'all cute and all, but I got work to do."

They laughed as Loretta backed away and let the two men into the house. Pete carried a small box and placed it on the table next to Maya.

"You remember my granddaughter, right?" Loretta asked Charles. Maya looked up from the piles she made with the gifts and waved.

"Yes, I do," Charles said, nodding at her, "but I don't think I had the pleasure of getting a name."

"Maya," she said absently, standing from the table. She stuck out her hand respectfully. "Nice to meet you."

"Likewise, young lady," he replied, his eyebrows raised in surprise. "Looks like you're busy."

"Yeah, Grams decided to be extra with the party this year."

"It's called details, child," Loretta corrected. "Trust me."

Charles and Pete laughed again.

"So, whatcha need done first?" Pete asked. "I brought a few decorations from the house that we didn't use. I figured you could use 'em."

"What is it?" Loretta asked.

"Just a few lights," he replied. "Maybe you can put them in the doorway or somethin'."

"That might be cute," Loretta said. "I have a mistletoe and some garland hanging over the kitchen doorway. Maybe we can put it there."

"I can help with that," Charles cut in.

"And why are you here, Mr. Charles?" Loretta inquired as she caught a glimpse of Maya trying to hold back a laugh. *Sweet eyes.*

"I came to supervise, but it looks like Pete might need some help, so," he replied holding out his hands in mock presentation, "here I am."

"My hero," Loretta said dryly.

During the next hour, the group transformed the living room into a festive party hall. Pete and Charles had rearranged the furniture to make room for dancing. Maya had completed the giftbags and after arranging them on the coffee table near the front door, had begun filming Loretta stringing lights while Pete and Charles argued about the best way to distribute the lighting to avoid an electrical surge.

Loretta found herself enjoying Charles's company, noticing his subtle winks and flirtations. Surprisingly, she had grown comfortable around him, and even found herself touching his shoulder when she laughed. She also noticed him watching her as if trying to figure her out. It didn't make her feel uncomfortable. Instead, it made her want to tell him more about herself. Too bad he would be returning to Houston soon. She could get used to this.

Myron arrived about a half hour later, but by that time, there was nothing left to do. Well, almost nothing.

"Let's set up a small bar by my wine cabinet," Loretta suggested. "Nothing too heavy. Just a few essentials like vodka, rum, stuff like that."

"Myron and I can run to the store and grab that for you," Maya said, rising from the table.

"Child, you are not twenty-one. I don't think so," Loretta said, shutting her down.

"It's okay, Miss Loretta," Myron said. "I'm twenty-two."

"Well, Maya is not," she shot back, drawing a groan from her granddaughter. Loretta didn't care. "I absolutely will not have my underaged granddaughter inside of a liquor store. I don't care who she's with. At least not on my watch."

Myron shrugged his shoulders in surrender. Fortunately, Pete stepped in to relieve the awkward moment.

"Uncle Charles and I can grab it for you real quick," he volunteered.

"Why don't you just order it?" Charles asked.

Loretta and Pete stared at him and asked in unison, "You can do that?"

"Come to think of it," Myron added, "there's an app you can use to order alcohol. My frat brothers used it for our Christmas kickback."

"What in the world is a kickback?" Loretta asked, and then dismissed the question. "Never mind. How do I order this alcohol? Won't they need an ID?"

"Now, how am I the oldest one in the room and the first one to think of this?" Charles asked with a laugh.

"Probably because you drink more than we do," Pete snapped.

Loretta laughed. "He got you there, old man."

"And I can still beat his young tail in an arm-wrestlin' match," Charles replied. He glared at his nephew and smiled. "Don't play with me, young buck."

The group exploded in laughter.

"On that note, we're gonna head out," Pete said with a smile, playfully pointing his thumb at the front door.

Charles scratched his ear. Loretta raised her eyebrow, sensing he was up to something. "Nephew, mind if I meet you later?"

"You good, Unc?" Pete asked.

"I'm good. I was just hopin' to take Miss Loretta for a walk before it gets too dark."

"Now, how you know I wanna go anywhere with you?" Loretta asked, playfully placing her hand on her hip.

"Woman, stop bein' difficult," Charles snapped, drawing snickers from Maya and Myron. "Now, can you change out those slippers so I can spend some time with you?"

"Guess you better do what he says, Grams," Maya said, propping her chin in her hand.

"I'm not leavin' you two alone in here," Loretta protested. "Liza would never let me hear the end of it."

"We're not gonna do anything, Grams," Maya assured her with a tinge of frustration. "In *your* house? That would be crazy."

"You shouldn't be doin' it at all," Loretta remarked, rolling her eyes.

"Relax, Loretta," Charles assured her, walking beside her. He glared at Myron so hard, the young man flinched. "I'm sure this young 'un knows anything he does to Maya, I'll do to him if he gets outta hand."

"He ain't lyin'," Pete added, still standing by the door. "I think y'all got this under control. I'll holler at y'all later."

Loretta smiled and raised her eyebrows at his flash of grandfather instinct. Meanwhile, Myron smiled nervously. "Y-you got nothin' to worry about."

Pete shot him a knowing smile and opened the door. "Uncle Charles, call me if you need me to pick you up later."

"I'll be alright," Charles said. "If it gets too late, I'll call a car."

"Well, I guess there's nothin' left for me to do except get my shoes," Loretta said with a shrug.

* * *

"You got a really beautiful family," Charles said as they strolled down the Lake Pontchartrain shore. "I like the way you and your granddaughter get along."

"She's my only grandbaby," Loretta replied, zipping her jacket closed as the New Orleans winter air brushed past her face. It wasn't freezing, but it was cooler than the New Orleans standard. "We always had a special relationship. She's smart and talented. I already know she's gonna go far."

"As you should," he said. They stared out over the water at a passing boat in the distance. "I don't think you have to worry about that young man she's keepin' time with. He seems like he's a good kid, too."

"I wouldn't know. I just met him on Christmas."

"I got a good feelin' about him."

"I'm glad you do," Loretta said, continuing to walk. "The jury's still out for me."

Charles smiled. "I told before, Miss Loretta. You a tough woman. I like that about you."

Loretta smiled slightly and looked away. "You say that a lot for somebody who's leavin' town in a couple days."

"You *do* know New Orleans is my home," he replied. "I just live in Houston. I'm a retired man who ain't attached to nobody. I can visit as much as I want."

"Then why do you live in Houston?"

"I like it there."

"Is that the only reason?"

Charles's face brightened as he took her hand. "Miss Loretta, if I wasn't careful, I would think you're askin' me to come back home."

Loretta laced her fingers with his and smiled back at him. "How could I ask that? I've only known you a few days."

"And you like me already."

Charles chuckled. "You know, you always ask me about who I'm seein' but you never talk about who you're seein'."

"That's because there's nobody to talk about," Loretta replied, averting her eyes. She hadn't lied. She didn't think Henri and Marcus were worth mentioning. But should she mention the dating app? She decided not to, reasoning it would be too much to explain.

They walked another few yards, the sun beginning to set. When Loretta noticed them getting further away from her usual turnaround point, she pulled Charles's hand toward her. "We'd better head on back."

He nodded and turned back, maintaining his grasp on her hand. Loretta looked down at their hands, her face warming. "Why did you say you never got married again?"

"Just easier," Charles said absently. "I like being able to do what I want without checkin' in."

"I guess I'm gonna be a problem."

"Why you say that?"

"If you got involved with me, you would have to communicate."

"That wouldn't be a problem," he remarked. They walked a few more feet and then he stiffened his arm, stopping her in her tracks. "For some reason, you make me wanna check in."

Loretta looked away, not knowing what to say next. Suddenly she felt a one-fingered caress along her left jaw. She looked up and Charles slowly lifted her chin, guiding her to look into his eyes. He leaned in closer, but before their lips could touch, Loretta's pocket rang.

"Sorry," she said, fiddling with the phone. When she saw Maya's name on the screen, dread filled her chest. Had something happened? "What's goin' on, Maya?"

"Nothin', we're good," Maya replied. "I was just lettin' you know my parents called and they're back home from work. Myron's gonna drive me back home."

"Alright, lemme know when you make it safe."

"I will. You need me to do anything before I leave?"

"Just leave the door unlocked," Loretta said, lowering her voice. "We'll be back soon."

"Okay, cool. Tell Mr. Charles we said hi."

"Hi, Maya!" Charles called. "Your timing is amazing."

"Huh?" Maya asked.

"Nothin', child," Loretta dismissed with a nervous laugh. "Just call me when you get home."

After hanging up with her granddaughter, Loretta looked back up at Charles, who watched her with a smirk.

"Saved by the bell, huh?"

"I guess so," she replied. "We'd better get back. It's gettin' darker."

They reached the house in nearly no time at all. Loretta couldn't shake the awkward feeling brought on by their almost kiss. She wanted to break away so she could process what had happened, but part of her wasn't ready for the evening to end.

"You – um – wanna come in for a drink while you wait for your car?" Loretta asked once reached the front door. "Or I can drive you home if you want."

"No, I'll order a car," he said, still holding her hand. "I don't want you drivin' by yourself if you ain't gotta."

"Well, aren't you protective," she remarked as she opened the door. Maya had done what she was told and had left the door unlocked. Loretta kicked off her tennis shoes and led Charles to the kitchen and offered him a seat at the bar. "I have some eggnog left if you'd like some."

"Homemade?" he asked as he sat.

"Of course. That store-bought stuff will never cross my doorframe."

Charles chuckled. "My kinda woman."

His words struck her. For some reason, he sounded just like James, who said those same words during their courting phase. She glanced up, wondering if James was trying to tell her something. She shook off the feeling and continued pouring the eggnog.

"You like yours warm?" she asked.

"Yeah, with a little brandy," he replied.

"That reminds me," she said, tapping her forehead. "I never placed that order."

"Have a seat and lemme show you how to do it," he offered.

"Okay, lemme warm these up a little," she replied, placing the two mugs in the microwave. As the forty-five seconds ticked by, she placed the last two pieces of pound cake in front of Charles. The microwave chimed, and she retrieved the mugs and set them on the bar. "Okay, show me how this works."

She pulled her phone from her pocket and followed Charles's instructions for downloading the app.

"Now enter your payment information and address here," he instructed, leaning closer to her. He smiled. "You smell good. I meant to tell you that earlier."

"Stop flirtin'," she scolded, pulling out her credit card. After adding her payment information to the app, she said, "We gotta get this done or else all y'all are gonna be drinkin' tomorrow night is punch."

Charles chuckled. "We can't have that."

He broke off a piece of pound cake and chased it down with a gulp of eggnog before taking her phone from her.

"I gotta give it to you," he said, pinching off another piece of cake. "This cake and eggnog are the best I ever tasted. Somethin' about homemade desserts."

She smiled in appreciation. "I'm glad you like it. These are my momma's recipes. I passed them down to my daughter, and Maya is learnin', too."

Charles nodded and smiled as they each pinched off the cake. He continued scrolling the app, selecting a few liquors he thought would be appropriate for the party.

"Make sure you order a few bottles of champagne. Or prosecco," Loretta said before sipping her eggnog.

"How many people you got comin' tomorrow?" he asked.

"Maybe twenty or so, but I like drinking mimosas with Liza and David on New Year's morning. It's kinda tradition."

Charles smiled and winked. "Maybe I can join y'all this year."

"You are bad," Loretta said with a giggle, tapping him on the shoulder.

He hit the order button and smiled. "Your alcohol will be here in the mornin'."

"Technology is an amazing thing," she remarked with a smile.

Just as she was about to take the phone from him, she heard a loud ding and a notification appeared at the top of the screen. Charles glanced down, his smiled dropping slightly. Loretta noticed the look and took the phone. She checked the notifications and found a message from Everett. She could almost feel the tension in the room shift.

He cleared his throat. "Didn't mean to pry."

Loretta shook her head. "It's fine."

Charles nodded, his smile totally gone. "Looks like you've got an admirer."

"Not really. Just somebody sendin' messages. Doesn't mean anything."

"Mm-hmm," Charles mumbled as he stood. "Well, I'll let you get back to it."

He pulled out his phone and did a few swipes and taps. "My car should be pullin' up in about ten minutes."

Loretta looked confused. "You okay?"

"Yeah, I'm good," he replied, remaining stoic as he walked to the door.

"What's wrong?" she asked as she followed him out.

He sighed and turned toward her. "Nothin'. I just don't think you're bein' totally honest with me. You keep askin' what I'm doin', but what are *you* doin'?"

She scrunched her eyebrows in confusion. "What do you mean, what *I'm* doin'?"

"Don't play dumb, Loretta."

"I don't think I'm the one playing, Charles. What are you talkin' about?"

Charles pursed his lips and stared at her. "First, it was the chef at the restaurant that you didn't bother to warn me about, and now I'm seein' messages on your phone."

"Stop being silly, Charles," Loretta snapped. "I don't need to keep secrets from you. We only met a few days ago."

"And I've been straight up with you the entire time. You too good to give me the same respect? Don't try to play me, Loretta."

"You're blowin' this all outta proportion."

"I don't think I am."

Loretta folded her arms and stared into his eyes. She couldn't believe the same eyes that almost drew her to kiss him earlier were now making her hate him. "You're bein' an old fool right now, you know that?"

"Again, with the name-callin'. Well, I'm just gonna take my old silly self out your house."

With that, he turned and walked out, barely mumbling a goodbye. Loretta stood there confused and a bit sad. She was starting to like Charles, and for the first time in a long time, she felt an attraction to someone other than James. And just like that, he was gone. All over an assumption and a misunderstanding.

Loretta peeked through the blinds and watched as Charles stood outside at the end of the driveway, his eyes glued to his phone. She guessed it would be another couple minutes before his Lyft got there. She'd keep watching until he was safely in the car. It was the least she could do.

Her phone chimed again. She looked down at her phone and was relieved to see that it was just a message from Liza.

Liza: *Just checking on you. Maya said you had company.*

Loretta grunted and typed, *Not anymore.*

Liza: *Well, I hope you had a good time. Mr. Charles seems nice.*

If you only knew, Loretta thought, again peeking through the blinds. Charles had just gotten into a car and closed the door, not even looking back at the house.

"I guess that's that," she groaned as she walked to her bedroom.

Chapter 12

The fight last night was still heavy on Loretta's mind as she trudged into the kitchen. As she waited for her coffee to brew, she glanced around, suddenly aware of how empty it felt. In a few hours, her home would be filled with family and friends, but for now, she was lonely.

She wanted to be mad at Charles. He'd made assumptions and had acted like a jealous child. He could have just asked instead of assuming she was seeing other people. It was just a text message. She had never even met Everett.

But then he also brought up Henri. Charles didn't know she never planned to see Henri again. He sure didn't mind slurping down that free wine Henri had sent them. But *now* he was a problem?

This was why she never wanted to date again after James had died. She really didn't know *how* to date. James had been her first love. She was only twenty-two years old when they married.

She had dated other boys before him, but they were just that— boys. She didn't take them seriously, and they probably hadn't taken her seriously. But James *saw* her. He knew what she needed before she even asked. He respected her, provided for her, and let her be … *her*.

"James, if this is your way of makin' sure I don't replace you, you coulda done it better than this," Loretta said aloud. "I wasn't gonna sleep with the man last night. You didn't have to run him off."

She chuckled to herself, and then her mind went back to Charles. In his own way, he'd had a point last night. She'd never fully told him how deeply she still felt for James, nor had she told him about Liza and Maya putting her on a dating app. When she saw Henri at the restaurant, she never told Charles how she knew him. And now Charles thought she was hiding something. She convinced herself she wasn't hiding anything, but she knew she hadn't been truly transparent. Maybe deep down, she didn't know what she was looking for. Maybe, just maybe, a forever bachelor living in Houston wasn't the answer.

She fished her phone from her pocket and searched it to find which day of Kwanzaa it was. She found it quickly. Kuumba, a day for using creativity to make the community more beautiful than how she'd found it.

"I think I do that every day," she mumbled, thinking back on her community work. "Heck, this party is part of that: bringing happiness to my family."

But could she do more? She'd have to think about that.

The doorbell rang, interrupting her thoughts. "Who in the world?"

She walked to the door and peeked through the blinds, a memory popping into her mind of Charles standing in her driveway last night. Two boxes sat on the porch near the door.

"Right," she said, lightly tapping her forehead. "I almost forgot about the alcohol."

She opened the door stared at the bottles sitting on her porch. She briefly considered leaving them there until someone else came over but dismissed the thought. Instead, she shuttled the bottles in herself, grabbing a couple at a time and placing them on the kitchen bar.

"At least that's done," she muttered, as she closed and locked the door. Charles's visit wasn't totally in vain.

Her phone rang as she walked back to the kitchen. She fished it from her pocket and was surprised to see Donovan Randall's name.

"Hey, Sister Willis," he greeted.

"Mornin', Brother Randall," she replied, sipping from her coffee. She frowned, realizing it had gotten cold. She placed the mug back on the counter, planning to make a new cup once she finished this call. "To what do I owe this pleasure?"

"I heard what happened last night," he said. "Charles is over here poutin' like a teenager."

Loretta sighed. "Brother Randall, I didn't start that. He saw one little text message and started jumpin' to conclusions."

He chuckled. "Charles is more sensitive than you might realize. He's just been through a lot. That divorce left a hole in him he never really patched up."

"We've all been through things," she said.

"I know, but we've been friends long enough for me to know your heart," he pushed. "You're a forgiving person. Don't let pride get in the way if you think there's somethin' there. Just the fact that he's over here poutin' shows me he really likes you. I ain't never seen him act like this."

"My momma used to tell me I had to suffer to be beautiful," Loretta said, tapping her foot. "She ain't never said I had to suffer for love."

"You one of the lucky ones," Donovan said. He sighed before continuing. "You and Brother Willis were together over forty years. Y'all went to church together every Sunday, and y'all got a beautiful daughter and granddaughter as a result. Charles ain't never had that. Sheila left him high and dry. Took half his money, cheated on him, lied to him. He never got over that. He claimed he never wanted to be vulnerable again, so he always ran at the first sign of conflict."

"So, what made me so different?"

"I don't know. Maybe you challenged him in a way other women couldn't."

Loretta's eyes traced the seam of the floor tiles as she thought about her friend's words. Was she ready to break down the walls of a man who was probably permanently set in his ways? Last week, she would have said no, but part of her wanted to explore Charles. She refused to try to fix him, but maybe if she could just understand him ....

"You still there, Sister Willis?" she heard him ask.

"I'm here," she said. "Just thinkin' about what you said."

"I'm not sayin' you gotta feel sorry for him, and I'm definitely not takin' sides. Just talk to him."

"He know you called me?"

"Heck, no! I know my brother, and he'd kill me if he knew I called you," he said with a laugh. "He's already decided not to come to your party tonight, talkin' 'bout he doesn't wanna be somewhere he ain't welcome. But I'm gonna work on him."

Loretta smiled faintly. "Well, we'll see. You're very convincing."

He laughed. "I'ma tell you like I told him: keep your heart open."

After they hung up, Loretta stood for a while, absently sipping from her coffee. She grunted, remembering it had gotten cold and immediately poured it into the sink. Kuumba again popped into her mind. Maybe this time creativity could mean finding new ways to heal.

* * *

"Cheryl," Liza called out to her assistant. "Can you look in Agility and pull up anything you can find on education reform?"

Her assistant sighed, but not subtly enough for Liza not to notice. She felt bad for making her work late on New Year's Eve, but she needed to complete this project. They were nearing the finish line, so it didn't make sense to let this go into the new year.

Liza clicked through her presentation, satisfied with the progress they'd made. The references from Cheryl would put the icing on the cake, and they could go into 2025 with a clean slate. Secretly, she felt guilty for taking Christmas Eve off. Maybe if she hadn't, they wouldn't be sitting in the office at 5:42 pm on New Year's Eve.

The last remnant of the sun had disappeared by the time Liza's phone rang. It could only be one person.

"Hey, hon," she greeted when she saw David's name flash on her phone screen. She stretched her back and shifted in her chair.

"You planning on coming home?" he asked.

"Of course," she replied, her eyes still glued to the computer screen. "I'm just trying to finish this project before the new year. We're almost done. I'll be home in time to change for the party, I promise."

He paused. "You've been workin' yourself into the ground. Ever since the day after Christmas, you've been goin' in early and comin' home late. When are you plannin' to get some rest?"

"I'm okay," she said without thinking. She froze. Cheryl's report had arrived, but all she could concentrate on were the words that had just left her mouth. Just a few days ago, she'd lamented on how her mother always said she was okay, even when she wasn't. After every event, after every long night cooking, after helping everyone but herself, she'd always say, "I'm okay."

Was Liza really okay? Or had she adopted her mother's martyr-like habits? No one really expected her to finish this report before January 1. She'd placed that expectation on herself. So why was she punishing herself and her assistant by burning up the last day of the year? Didn't she have a party to go to? Her mother's party, no less.

Liza sat back, suddenly exhausted. Not just physically, but spiritually. She had spent the whole year trying to be the perfect executive, the perfect wife, the perfect mother, and the perfect daughter. She refused to go into 2025 with the same mindset. It was time to make space to just be herself.

"Babe, I'll be home shortly," she said, closing the presentation. "Let's get ready to party."

* * *

Maya held up two pairs of earrings to her ears, both sparkly, both doing way too much. It was New Year's Eve, but, she was only going to Grams' house. Did she really need to dress like she was going to the club?

She sighed and decided on the gold hoops. Myron was coming, so she needed to make sure she looked good. She wasn't sure how far she and Myron would go, but she was enjoying the ride. Smart, respectful, and had a body like Michael B. Jordan and teeth like Omarion. He was a little nerdy, but she liked that. At least she didn't have to worry about him trying to be a player.

Even with all those attributes, her father still didn't trust Myron, and for the life of her, Maya couldn't understand why. Myron had never done anything to make her father dislike him the way he did. Sure, they'd messed around and had even spent nights together during the semester, but her dad didn't know that.

Maya sighed. Her dad wouldn't have to worry about her boyfriend much longer. Yesterday, Myron had informed her that he was considering going to California after graduating at the end of the upcoming semester. She was sure they wouldn't withstand a long-distance relationship. The thought made her sad, but she refused to dwell on it tonight. It was New Year's Eve. She could worry about breakups in a few months.

She looked into her mirror as she clipped on the hoops. They framed her face just right, perfectly complimenting her soft high afro puff and two curls that cascaded down the sides of her face. She freshened her gold lipstick, which stood out from her glossy soft-glam makeup that had a touch of gold shimmer. She'd copied the look from her favorite makeup guru on YouTube, and even if she said so herself, she'd done a great job.

Her bedroom looked like Hurricane Katrina had whipped through it. Her pink frilly dress hung neatly on her closet door, but the outfits she'd decided against were strewn all over her bed while her makeup brushes, shoes, and hair products were scattered across her desk and floor. In the corner, her phone was propped on its ring light, recording a time-lapse of her getting ready so she could use it for content later.

She walked over to the ring light and pressed the square stop button. After taking the phone from its holder, she stared into the screen and searched for the best light to snap a few selfies.

Satisfied with the light from the setting sun shining through the window, she smiled, threw up the peace sign, and snapped a few photos.

Impulsively, she checked the comments on her latest reel featuring Grams with her beautiful fluffy afro. The engagement was still rising, but her eyes landed on a string of negative comments.

KLove: *Ain't nothin special about this hairdo.*
Mikki_B34: *I agree. If it wasn't for her grandmother, this whole post would be mid.*

Maya rolled her eyes. She knew negativity came with the territory for influencers, but it hit differently when it was directed at her. She continued reading and smiled when she saw a few comments defending her.

VickiT: *I wouldn't be talking. Judging from your profile pic, you could use this girl's help.*
FreeFreddie817: *There always gotta be a hater in the bunch.*
CooperS: *Y'all just wish you looked as good as this girl's grandma.*

Maya giggled, responding to a few of the positive comments and ignoring the negative ones. She was glad her grandmother was able to help with her following, but it was time for her audience to realize Loretta wouldn't always be the star of the show. Maya had her own hairstyles to display, and when she started school in a couple weeks, she'd be showcasing her friends' hair. If she played this right, she could make enough money to make a down payment on her own car. Maybe even take a trip to see Myron at the end of the schoolyear.

Maya smiled and nodded at the possibilities.

Her friend Abby was a successful influencer. When the semester started, she'd try to get some advice from her. In the meantime, she posted a selfie accompanied by a Happy New Year and the hashtags:

#bayoucutie
#newyearflow
#goldenglow
#newyearnewpossibilities

"Maya!" David called from the next room.

"Yes, Dad?" Maya answered dryly, slightly annoyed at the interruption of her thoughts. She walked to her door and looked out into the hallway. David was nowhere to be seen, which meant he must have been in his room. She rolled her eyes and wilted a little, knowing if she went back into her room, she'd have a hard time hearing him. Instead, she walked to her parents' bedroom and talked to him through the door.

"Your momma's gonna be home in about an hour. You about ready?" he asked.

"I stay ready!"

"Yeah, alright. Just be ready to leave her when she gets here. She won't take long to get ready."

"Yeah, right."

She went back to her room and closed her door before her father could respond. Sometimes she felt she knew her mother better than he did. In no universe did she ever get dressed quickly.

Since she still had her phone in hand, she sat on her bed and texted Myron to remind him what time he should meet her at the party. Instead of waiting for him to reply, she walked to her desk and picked up her rattail comb and styling gel and reshaped her baby hairs. Once she finished, she stood back and admired her work.

"Okay, you cute!" she said aloud, blowing her reflection a kiss.

Her phone dinged. She scooped up her phone from her desk and found a message from Myron saying he would be there.

"You better be," she mumbled.

She slipped on her dress. After giving herself one more mirror inspection, she placed the phone back on her ring light, positioned it to pick up the best light, and hit record.

"Hey, what's up, y'all, it's your girl, Maya, also known as the Bayou Cutie," she announced, posing with her hands on her hips. "I know y'all are probably getting dressed for the New Year. As you can see, I am, too. I'm heading to my Grams' New Year's Eve party. Y'all seen her. She ain't no ordinary grandma.

"Before everybody heads out and brings in the new year, I just wanted to take a second to thank y'all for all the support over the past few days. I started doin' this because my momma wanted me to get a job, but I wanted to do somethin' I love. I've been doin' hair since high school. I love natural hair. It's magic! And if I could pursue my passion while makin' my momma happy, I think that's a win!"

She giggled a little. "I'm jokin', y'all. Well, kind of. So, a little about me: I'm from New Orleans, and I'm a sophomore pre-med major at Dillard University. So yeah, your girl is headed to med school in a couple years. If this social media thing works out, I won't need student loans, and y'all gonna be callin' me Dr. Maya with the bangin' twist-out!

"I really didn't think anybody would care about my page, but when I posted my Grams, y'all went crazy. I had done her hair and showed it to the world. After that, I knew we were lookin' at somethin' big! I thank y'all for that. Not just for supportin' my page, but for helpin' Grams see the light in her that I saw. Y'all shoulda seen the way her smile and energy went up. She was really feelin' herself! Hair really holds emotion and heritage, and y'all proved it that day."

She moved closer to the camera, encouraged when she saw the encouraging comments climb up the screen.

"Today is the sixth day of Kwanzaa, known as Kuumba, or creativity. It hit me that this channel and even this video are all part of me honoring that principle. I'm using my creativity to uplift, to share, and to grow. And we're keepin' that energy in 2025. My Grams will still make an occasional appearance but we're also gonna talk about haircare, mental health, and education. And for the young girls who have questions about med school and college life, don't be afraid to hit your girl up.

"Y'all ready to level up together? Drop down in the comments and let me know how you're levelin' up in 2025."

She smiled and chuckled a little.

"I know it may seem crazy that I'm dressed like this to go to my Grams' house, but like I said, she's no ordinary grandma. She constantly shows up for people even when she's tired, and she's poured into everyone in this family, and even a few people who aren't family. Because of her—and a little help from bae—I'm about to blow this last semester of my sophomore year out the water. Straight A's. Dean's List. Believe that.

"Happy New Year, y'all. I'll be back later tonight for the countdown."

She winked and shot the camera a concluding smile before turning it off.

"Maya!" Liza called. "We're leavin' in ten minutes!"

Chapter 13

Girl, I just don't think I'm cut out for this datin' thing," Loretta said as she and Mavis put the finishing touches on her beautifully decorated living room. The Christmas tree lights and the lights from the mistletoe over the kitchen doorway sparkled like a magical wonderland, and soft R&B music piped through the speakers.

She was thankful her sorority sister had decided to come early. Because of her, the bar had been set up, and the caterer had set the meal up on the dining table in a configuration that would rival the fanciest restaurants in the Central Business District.

"I think it's kinda nice you tried to get out there," Mavis replied, pinching off a piece of the roasted chicken. Loretta was about to fuss at her friend for picking at the food, but she couldn't blame her. She'd been eyeballing that chicken, herself.

"I might have to get on the app, myself," Mavis continued. "Being old and alone is for the birds."

"Yeah, but some of these men deserve to be alone. Remember I told you about Henri?"

Mavis laughed. "How can I forget? He was a character."

"Exactly."

"Too bad it didn't work out with your handyman's uncle. What was his name?"

"Charles," Loretta groaned. She felt a pit in her stomach just from the mention of his name. She wasn't ready to admit she missed him.

"Yeah, that's it," Mavis said, nodding as she pinched another piece of the chicken."

"Girl, you keep sneakin' pieces of that chicken, ain't gon' be none left!"

Mavis sucked the chicken juices from her thumb and smiled. "Have you tasted this? Your chef did his thing! Henri could never with his vegan gumbo-makin' self."

Loretta yelped in laughter. "That vegan gumbo wasn't half bad."

"I'll let you tell it. I refuse to try it."

Loretta was thankful for her friend's humor, but she couldn't totally expel thoughts of Charles from her mind. The feeling irritated her because she hadn't known him long enough for him to have taken residence in her thoughts. This type of vulnerability was out of order.

Yet, before Mavis arrived, she'd checked her phone more times than she cared to admit. Charles hadn't called or texted. Brother Randall said he'd handle it, but she guessed he failed. Why should she care? She hadn't had a date for New Year's Eve since James had died. This year would be no different.

"Well, too bad Charles had to act a fool," Mavis said, saving Loretta from her thoughts. "He's just gonna have to miss how good you look, 'cause girl, you wearin' that outfit!"

"Awww, thank you, Soror," Loretta said with a smile and a twirl. Her black and red dress with a sequined top fit perfectly. Maya had silk pressed her hair earlier that day, styling it into a sleek silver and black world of curls, and her makeup was flawless. "You're lookin' good, too."

Mavis placed her hands on her hips and struck a pose, displaying her black sequined jumpsuit. She looked great, although Loretta thought it was a bit much. But who was she to judge when she was wearing sequins, herself?

"Your company should be arriving soon," Mavis said, checking her watch. "Lemme go use the restroom and check my makeup. Maybe I'll luck up and somebody'll bring a lonely eligible bachelor to the party."

Loretta laughed as her friend walked to the bathroom, but deep down, the only lonely eligible bachelor she wanted to see at the party was Charles. She scrunched her face and cut her eyes at her cell phone, which sat peacefully on the dining room table next to the shrimp pasta. She then looked at the bathroom door to make sure it was closed.

Before she could talk herself out of it, she snatched her phone from the table and dialed Charles's number. He answered on the second ring. "Hey."

"Hey yourself," she said softly, sitting on the sofa. "I wasn't sure if you'd pick up."

"I almost didn't."

Loretta winced. "I just wanted to say Happy New Year. Your brother said you weren't comin'."

"He said right."

She sighed. "I know it hasn't been that long since we started spendin' time, but I thought maybe—"

"Maybe what?" he snapped. "Maybe we could pretend you keep buildin' walls between us? Pretend I'm just gonna go back to Houston and forget about you? You keep sayin' I'm the one with baggage, but woman, you got 'em, too."

She said nothing.

"You keep tellin' me I gotta be honest," he continued, "but I don't even know who I'm competin' with. I know you're not obligated to me, but I can't be the only one layin' it all out."

"It wasn't like that," Loretta whispered.

"I know you think that," he replied. "You think I'm the one not ready, but it's you. And that's okay. But I saw something in you, Loretta. Still do. Just too bad you don't see it with me."

He hung up without another word. She sat still. Her heart ached. She closed her eyes. When she opened them, Mavis was standing there.

"You okay, Soror?" she asked softly.

Loretta stood and gave her a half-hearted smile. "Girl, I'm not about to let that man ruin my new year."

"It's okay if you do," Mavis said. "This is your first time likin' a man since James died. It's new territory for you."

"Who says I like him?" Loretta snapped. "I am *good*!"

"If you say so," Mavis agreed without conviction. "I just want you to be happy."

"I'm happy, Soror," Loretta assured her. "Lemme go freshen up. Liza should be here soon."

Before Mavis could say anything else, Loretta made a beeline for her bedroom, closing her door behind her. The tears threatened to show themselves, but she refused to let them flow in front of Mavis. Instead, she sat on her bed and allowed a lone tear to streak her eyeliner.

She reached over to her nightstand and pulled a tissue from the drawer. As she dabbed at the tear, she felt a presence standing over her. She looked up and gasped.

"James," she whispered.

He looked good, wearing a sleek black suit with velvet lapels as if he was ready to escort her to the party himself. An aura of light surrounded him, giving him a glow. He smiled at her and gently tugged her earlobe like he used to do when he needed her to listen.

"Why you scared?" he asked.

"I'm not scared."

He chuckled. "This is me you're talkin' to. Baby, we had forty-three beautiful years together. You don't have to spend the rest of your life by yourself just to prove you still love me. I already know that. And stop usin' your age as an excuse not to date. You're too beautiful to not be happy."

Loretta blinked back tears. "I'm tired, James. Real tired."

"I know. But you're still here. And you deserve more than being alone at your own party and pretendin' you're okay. You don't always have to be strong. That's what's makin' you tired. It's worth seein' if that fella can give you some rest."

She looked at him and smiled, the first genuine smile she'd had since yesterday. "You sure, my love?"

James smiled and winked. "I'm sure. I already know you ain't gon' neva love him like you loved me. And if he breaks your heart, I'ma haunt his tail 'til he dies."

She giggled. "Thank you, James."

A knock at the door jolted her. She looked around. James was gone, but the feeling he'd given her was still there.

"Loretta?" Mavis called through the door. "Your friend Donovan and his family are here."

Could Charles be with him? "Okay, I'll be out in a minute. Almost done."

Loretta scampered to her bathroom and checked the mirror. Her makeup was smeared, but a few swipes of concealer and foundation and some fresh eyeliner, and it was like nothing had ever happened.

By the time Loretta had made it back to the living room, Liza, Maya, and David were walking through the door. A quick glance told her Charles wasn't there, but she managed to put on a brave face and greet her guests.

"Sister Willis, you look beautiful," Sister Randall complimented. "I love your dress."

"You're lookin' good yourself," Loretta replied with a smile.

"I really tried with that turkey," Donovan whispered as he hugged Loretta.

"Don't even worry about it," she dismissed. "His loss."

After greeting Pete and his wife, Loretta walked over to Liza and hugged her. "You worked late, didn't you?"

"What else is new?" Liza admitted. "Sorry I couldn't help you earlier."

"Don't worry, that's what friends are for," Loretta replied, looking over at Mavis, who was already pouring herself a drink.

"Where's Mr. Charles?" Liza asked, looking around. "Is he comin'?"

"Nope," Loretta replied curtly. She walked away before Liza could say anything else.

By eleven, the house was alive with the sound of laughter and glass clinking. The food was a hit, and everyone wore at least one thing from the gift bags Maya had packed.

Loretta waded through the crowd, greeting and laughing with her guests, but finding herself glancing at the door in hopes that Charles had changed his mind. She refused to show sadness, smiling graciously and even doing the Wobble with Maya and Myron. Pete and his wife cheered and joined them, followed by David and Liza.

Midnight crept closer, but there was still no Charles.

"You good, Soror?" Mavis asked. She wore oversized glasses and a glittery gold hat that made Loretta chuckle.

"I'm great," Loretta responded. "The party turned out better than expected.

"It did," Mavis replied, "but don't think I didn't notice you starin' at the door."

"Just a force of habit," Loretta replied. "Let's pour the champagne. It's almost midnight."

She led Mavis to the kitchen and pulled a package of plastic champagne flutes from the cabinet. As she assembled them and set them on the kitchen table, Mavis popped a bottle of champagne and began filling the flutes.

"You sure can give a party," Mavis commented as she popped open another bottle.

"I enjoy it."

At ten minutes before midnight, Liza helped Mavis and Loretta pass out the champagne flutes. Loretta then turned off the music and turned the television to *Dick Clark's New Year's Rockin' Eve with Ryan Seacrest*. She preferred Dick Clark. New Year's just hadn't been the same since he passed.

The clock ticked closer to midnight. Loretta stood in the kitchen doorway as the party guests gathered to watch the TV.

"Here we go!" Maya announced as the countdown started.

"Ten!"

"Nine!"

A sudden sense of regret hit Loretta as reality set in that this would be the first year she would unwillingly spend New Year's Eve alone. She smiled through it, not wanting anyone feeling sorry for her.

"Eight!"

Maybe it's best this way, she thought. She barely knew the man.

"Seven!"

"Six!"

"Five!"

She tapped her fingernails against her flute as she saw Brother and Sister Randall embrace, getting ready for the big moment. David and Liza did the same, followed by Pete and his wife and her in-laws. Even Myron respectfully hugged Maya. Loretta stood alone.

"Four!"

"Three!"

She took a deep breath, ready for the gallons of sap about to spill all around her.

"Two!"

"One! Happy New Year!"

Cheers and horns sounded throughout the room. Loretta lifted her champagne flute and was about to shout Happy New Year once more, but someone grabbed her waist and spun her around. She gasped when she faced him, but before she could say anything, his lips met hers with a long-awaited kiss.

More cheers erupted, combining with the cheers and Auld Lang Syne coming from the television. Liza ran up and swept them both into a tight hug. "Now, that's how you bring in a new year! Y'all cute!"

Loretta just stared in stunned silence, barely acknowledging her daughter's words. "Are you serious? Whatcha doin' here? I thought you weren't comin'?"

He smiled. "I almost didn't, but I couldn't let the year end without seeing you."

She took a deep breath. "I'm glad you did."

"Are you really?"

She hugged him, a lone tear slipping from her closed eyes. "I don't know what it is about you."

"It's about time you came to your senses!" Brother Randall said, slapping Charles on the back.

"And right under the mistletoe you insisted on helpin' with," Pete added with a laugh.

Loretta and Charles looked up and laughed when they saw the sparkling lights and red mistletoe hanging above them.

"Couldn't have planned it any better," Mavis chimed in.

Charles took Loretta's hands into his and kissed her again. "I know we just met each other, but we're gettin' old. I ain't tryna date you for no two, three years, and I ain't tryna play no games. I ain't lettin' you get away from me, Loretta Willis, so you gon' have to tell your lil boyfriends you taken now."

"Talk that talk, big man!" Myron shouted, drawing laughs from the other guests.

"I told you he was smooth," Maya added, pointing her phone toward her grandmother.

Loretta's face turned red with embarrassment after noticing she was being recorded. She blinked at her granddaughter and then turned her attention back to Charles. "What about Houston?"

"You let me handle that," Charles told her. "Just keep givin' me a reason to come back. Can you handle that?"

Loretta swallowed and looked around, feeling the prying eyes of every guest resting on her. She had not expected to start 2025 this way, but she had to admit she was glad she had. Why not take a chance? She nodded, and the entire party broke out in applause.

"That's what I'm talkin' 'bout!" Charles exclaimed, pulling Loretta into another hug.

She let herself melt into his arms, and for the first time since James died, she felt comfortable. Finally, she felt ready.

Epilogue

The scent of fried smoked sausage and coffee intermingled with the possibilities of the final day of Kwanzaa—Imani—made New Year's Day extra sweet. Liza turned on the smooth jazz station and then began mixing the waffles, singing along with Sade's Cherish the Day, the perfect song to usher in the principle of faith.

Spending the night at her mother's house only made sense. She and her family had done so for the past six years, mostly because no one felt like driving across the city at one in the morning. Liza had grown to enjoy the sleepovers and had recently begun waking up early to cook breakfast and make mimosas.

She smiled as she moved around the kitchen, slightly glad she was the only one up and could have a little time to herself. She didn't get much of it, especially since work had become more demanding. She knew she was stretching herself too thin, but at this point, she really had no idea how to stop.

A sudden shuffle of feet behind her broke her thoughts. She turned to see Maya walking in, still in her satin bonnet and slippers.

"Morning, Ma," Maya said, walking up to Liza and giving her a tight hug. "Need any help?"

"I always need help," Liza said tossing a dishtowel at her daughter. "You're up early."

Maya smiled and yawned. "I smelled sausage and figured I'd come pretend help so I could sneak a few pieces."

Liza laughed. "Well, you won't be pretendin'. Grab the eggs and get to scramblin'."

Maya giggled and did as she was told. One by one, she expertly cracked the eggs into a small mixing bowl, emulating a technique she once saw on TikTok. "Grams up yet?"

"I haven't seen her," Liza replied, pulling out the waffle maker from the pantry. She set it on the counter next to the stove and plugged it in. "I think I crashed before all of y'all, so I haven't seen anyone since the party."

"Yeah, I think Daddy went to sleep not long after you did. Myron left around one and then I went to sleep on the couch. I think Grams was still in the den with Mr. Charles by the time I dozed off."

"Charles sure did his thing last night," Liza said with a smirk.

"He sure did, and I got most of it recorded."

"I thought I saw you recording last night. You better not post that without your grandmother's permission."

Maya shook her head as she mixed the eggs with a whisk. "I wouldn't do that to her. She was so embarrassed, but she also looked happy."

"She did, didn't she?"

Well, I know the online dating thing didn't work out, but in a way I'm glad we did it. It helped her be more open to finding love again. She deserves it."

"I agree," Maya said.

"Agree with what?" David asked, walking into the kitchen wearing a Xavier University T-shirt and a pair of basketball short. He walked straight to the coffee pot, kissed Liza's cheek, and took a mug from the cabinet. After making his coffee, he leaned against the cabinet.

"We were just takin' credit for Grams finding love," Maya joked as she turned on the fire under the cast iron skillet.

David laughed. "Y'all a trip. I think Momma Loretta got Charles all by herself. Y'all had nothin' to do with it."

"That's not the way I'm gonna tell the story," Liza quipped, spraying cooking spray inside the waffle maker.

"Of course not," David said, shaking his head.

"By the way, you two," Maya cut in, changing the subject, "I just want to thank you both."

Liza turned to her. "For what?"

"For supporting my page and not laughing when I said I wanted to take it seriously. It means a lot."

Liza pat her daughter on the shoulder and then squeezed it. "Baby, I'll always support you. If you're willing to be consistent, I'll always have your back. But you're still plannin' on bein' a doctor, right?"

"Absolutely," Maya nodded. "This page is just going to help finance some things so I don't have to keep askin' you for money. I really believe I can do something with this."

"I don't know much about how all that works, but I have seen the work you're putting into it," David said. "Just make sure it lasts longer than your winter vacation and make it sure it doesn't get in the way of school."

"I promise," Maya vowed. "I'm going to make a content calendar to help me stay consistent. I can't keep depending on Grams for my videos."

Liza laughed. "She *is* a scene-stealer. Well, I'm proud of you. Stick with it."

"What y'all in here talkin' about?" Loretta asked, appearing in the doorway. She wore a black warm-up suit, and her hair was pulled into a bun. Her face said she hadn't slept a wink.

Maya tried to suppress a grin. "Morning, Grams. You look *rested*."

Loretta waved her off. "Don't start."

"Quite a night, huh?" Liza said, shooting her mother a smile.

"Sure was," Loretta mumbled, pouring herself a cup of coffee.

"You want a mimosa?" Liza asked.

Loretta nodded. "Soon as I finish my coffee."

She looked around the kitchen and watched as Liza poured batter into the waffle maker. "Thanks for startin' breakfast. Doesn't look like y'all need my help."

"Nope, we got it," Maya said as she mixed the eggs into the skillet.

"Your girls have been up for a minute," David said before sipping his coffee.

"Well, I guess I'll sit myself down," Loretta said, taking a seat at the bar next to David.

A soft digital chime interrupted the family's banter. Maya scampered to the living room and came back smiling at her phone.

"Myron texted to say Happy New Year like he didn't just see me last night," she bragged with a girlish giggle.

"He really likes you, huh?" Loretta asked.

She cut her eyes at David when he grumbled, "We'll see."

"Seems like it," Maya replied, sticking her phone in her pocket and making a face at her dad. "Last night he told me Mr. Charles inspired him."

"Loretta looked confused. "How so?"

"He told me that watching Mr. Charles last night made him rethink moving to California," Maya explained. "He said if things keep workin' out for us this semester, maybe we could either try long distance or he could look at grad schools closer to home. I guess Mr. Charles's vow of love rubbed off on him."

Liza turned. "Vow of love?"

Loretta sucked her teeth and shook her head. "Ain't nobody vowed nothin'."

"Did I hear somebody say my name?" Charles asked, rubbing his eyes as he walked into the kitchen wearing the same pants from last night and a wrinkled shirt that hung halfway out his waistband.

Liza blinked. "Wait ... *he spent the night*?"

David chuckled, setting down his mug. "Mind your business, babe."

Loretta pretended to be unbothered. "It was late, we needed to talk, and one thing led to another. Now he's here."

Charles wrapped an arm around her shoulders. "I'm staying a few more days. Thought Loretta and I could actually explore this thing before we both run off scared again."

Liza scrunched her eyebrows and cocked her head to the right. "Um, what is happening here?"

"Two grown folks, well over twenty-one, who are mindin' our own grown folks' business," Loretta said with a smile.

"Y'all serious, huh?" Maya asked.

Charles nodded. "I don't know what the future holds, but I know I don't wanna let her get away."

Loretta looked at him and blinked. "That was some talk you and your brother had."

"Can I be honest?" Charles asked, pulling his arm away and sitting across from her. Liza caught a look of concern flush over her mother's face but remained silent. "It was actually your friend Mavis who convinced me."

"Mavis? How?" Loretta asked with a look of confusion. Liza nearly dropped the waffle she pulled from the waffle maker as she leaned in to hear more.

"Well, after you called me last night, you musta left your phone on," he explained. "She called me as soon as you left the room and lit into me. Told me I was a fool, and that it took a lot for you to call me. My brother had pretty much told me the same thing, but I guess it hit different comin' from her, so I came over. I didn't mean to make that grand entrance, but that's just how it turned out."

"Well, I'll be," Loretta remarked. "That darn Mavis."

"You've got a good friend," Maya said.

"Yeah, I'ma have to take her out one of these days."

"And speakin' of takin' people out," David interjected, rising from his seat at the bar. "I hope y'all aren't making any plans for Liza next month."

Liza raised an eyebrow. "Why?"

"Because I'm takin' you on vacation."

Liza blinked. "You're what?"

"Baby, you're always takin' care of everybody else, and I'm tired of you puttin' yourself on the backburner. Now, your report is done, Maya has some direction, and your momma got a man."

"Excuse me?" Loretta asked.

"Yeah, how did we catch a stray in your lil speech?" Maya snapped.

"Can y'all let me finish?" he asked, glaring at Loretta and Maya as Charles chuckled. He turned back to Liza, and she smiled. "It's your turn to relax, so I decided last night to take you someplace sunny next month. No phones, mothers, or daughters allowed."

Liza looked at him, stunned. "You're serious?"

"As a heart attack."

Liza squealed in excitement and clapped her hands. "Do I get to pick the place?"

"Nope! Just let me do this."

"Controlling women run in this family, don't they?" Charles remarked.

"You don't know the half," David replied, shaking his head.

"Well, I think this calls for a mimosa," Loretta suggested, opening the refrigerator and grabbing the orange juice. Once everyone—even Maya—had poured a glass, Loretta lifted hers. "To new beginnings."

"To choosing yourself," David added.

Liza smiled at him. "To family."

"To facing your fears," Charles said, smiling at Loretta.

"To finding yourself," Maya whispered.

As they sat together and enjoyed their breakfast, Liza realized the year 2025 would be filled with a walk of faith. What started as a sneaky way to take her mother's happiness into her own hands had possibly changed the course of their lives for the better. What a way to begin the year!

The End

About the Author

Dr. Rhonda M. Lawson is a twenty-five-time published author, retired US Army Master Sergeant, and the visionary founder of Meet the World Image Solutions, a literary and publicity firm dedicated to helping authors become powerful storytellers and industry experts. With more than 30 years of writing, editing, and strategic communication experience, Dr. Rhonda brings a rare blend of military precision, journalistic clarity, and creative passion to every project.

As a book coach and editor, she has worked with hundreds of authors to turn their ideas into well-crafted, publishable manuscripts, many of which have become fan favorites and award winners. Her specialties include VIP coaching, done-for-you publishing, and high-impact publicity campaigns that position her clients for long-term success.

Dr. Rhonda is also the creator and host of Horizons Author Lounge, a weekly author showcase that has introduced audiences to emerging voices and bestselling writers alike. Her signature event, the Black History Month Literary Weekend, celebrates

Black literature, authorship, and scholarship through book signings, workshops, and student outreach across the country.

A native of New Orleans now based in the DMV area, Dr. Rhonda combines Southern charm with no-nonsense guidance. She's passionate about making writing fun again and ensuring that authors, especially those from underrepresented communities, have access to the tools and visibility they need to succeed.

Whether she's on stage, behind the scenes, or coaching a new writer through their first draft, Dr. Rhonda is dedicated to turning passion into purpose. Learn more about Dr. Rhonda and her books and services at www.mtwimagesolutions.com.

Join the Write to Win Writers Community

Did you love this book?

Do you have your own story to tell?

Why not join the *Write to Win Writers Community* on Skool? I created this space for aspiring and established authors who are ready to write boldly, build visibility, and WIN. Inside, you'll find:

- Weekly writing resources
- Monthly workshops & challenges
- AI tools made just for authors
- Real-time support and a tribe that *gets you*

Whether you're working on your first book or your fifteenth, there's a seat for you at the table. Visit https://www.mtwimagesolutions.com/write-to-win-writers-community for more info!

Follow me at:
Instagram: @meettheworldimagesolutions
Facebook: @ MTWImageSltns
YouTube: @meettheworldimagesolutions
TikTok: @DrRhondaL

Let's make this *your* writing season!